U0059159

米家路中英對照詩選

Collected Poems of Mi Jialu 1981-2018

Deep Breaths

深呼吸

謹以此詩卷獻給我最親愛的家人

內子盧丹
愛女米顆
愛子米稻

名家推薦

　　《深呼吸》是一本別致的詩集，其中的詩十分純粹。它們表現了詩人獨具的品格：敏感、沉靜、超脫卻又執著。書頁中還常常散發著淡雅的氣韻。

——哈金（著名小說家，詩人，美國國家圖書獎獲得者，
美國藝術文學院院士，波士頓大學英文系教授）

　　米家路的詩集《深呼吸》並非偶然。那是一個修行了三十七年「深呼吸」的詩人，加上純淨的靈魂洗禮，而終於產生的一種穿越時空的精心成果。顯然如此真誠又專注的米家路就是他詩中所說的那位詩人：「策馬／千里迢迢／與大道競跑／呼吸／迎風撲面的顫慄／那是繆斯的呼召」。此外，書中幾位英譯者都十分傑出，所以讀這本中英對照的詩集，確實是一種享受。

——孫康宜（耶魯大學　Malcolm G. Chace'56東亞語文講座教授，
中央研究院院士）

　　流離是二十世紀以來中國人的宿命，一個有詩心的知識份子更是如此，所幸米家路隨身攜帶的漢語照亮了他的遠遊，深呼吸帶來的，是語言的靜謐。

——廖偉棠（著名詩人，文化評論家）

　　抒情，已是華語詩的基調，自《詩經》到現代詩的傳承，我欣喜閱讀到米家路這本《深呼吸》詩集，能利用不同的句型、西方詩的格式、具有哲思的文字感，塑造出他個人風格的作品。離開主流場域，

隔離熱鬧的搶話語權的場子，行腳或停居於東西方大地，米家路這本
《深呼吸》詩集，在品讀之後，感受到詩人掙脫學術圈僵硬的語彙，
有別於大陸詩壇亂哄哄的喊口號，他融合中國與西方文學語境，將其
一生的曲折、見識、遭遇、感悟，化為一行行一篇篇精緻的詩作，因
此推薦給那些還在尋覓好的抒情詩集者，打開它，看米家路的詩，來
一次心靈的深呼吸吧。

——顏艾琳（著名詩人，跨界策劃人）

　　米家路詩歌中的純粹抒情在現今的詩裡已經相當罕見了。即使在
具有強烈敘事性的段落或篇章裡，也充滿了抒情性的純淨氣息，令人
讚嘆。遠離中國的空間距離使得米家路在寫作上避免了當前漢語詩歌
的各種現有模式或匠氣，堅持了自己獨有的鮮活風格。作為一位造詣
深厚的文化／文學學者，米家路這次用感性的語言說話，讓我們獲得
了漢語的非凡敞亮感。

——楊小濱（著名詩人，中央研究院中國文哲所研究員，
文化評論家）

詩集編輯說明與致謝

　　《深呼吸》詩集收錄了筆者跨度三十七年的詩歌創作，大多數作品均首次從幽暗的箱底翻躍出來見光面世，彷彿深深呼一口氣，感歎，「活著真好！見光真好！」筆者真沒想到對詩歌深吸的那一口原氣居然存活了三十七年的星際旅程，猶如潛隱江湖的苦行僧，在岩層底下默默修行，無關世事紛爭，既刻苦銘心體悟真道，又隨遇而安漫步生命歷程，所以這部詩集與其說是呈現詩歌某些高超精湛的神祕技藝，還不如說是作者奉獻給廣大讀者那口恒而持久的，鍥而不捨的修行魅力與心靈真氣。幾十年來筆者從來沒有沽名釣譽去妄稱自己為詩人，而僅僅自視為一位貪戀詞語的雜耍手而已。

　　依照心靈歷程的倒敘閃回次序，本詩集分成三個部分：第一部分《天涯離騷1996-2018》涵蓋了筆者自1996年負笈到加州大學大衛斯分校留學與從2002年任教於新澤西學院至今以來所寫的作品，袒露了筆者海外漂泊離散的複雜心路。

　　第二部分《望氣歌樂山1985-1995》涵蓋了筆者人生的三個階段：1985年大學畢業後留校任教於歌樂山麓下的四川外語學院，1988至1991年上北京大學攻讀比較文學碩士研究生和1993至1996年南下香港中文大學留學。這北上南下的遊學十年便是筆者詩歌氣場吸收與漲潮的歲月。

　　第三部分《青春流光1981-1984》收錄了筆者在歌樂山下川外念本科時所寫的青春期作品。這些初道之作稚嫩，粗陋，但卻真誠可愛，仍是可追溯的生命蹤跡與初始呼吸，權作存念吧！

　　這部詩集是中英文雙語對照，筆者有幸得到以下諸位傑出翻譯家的大力支持，他們抽出寶貴的時間在短短的幾個月裡就完成了英譯，雖然譯文最後均由筆者數次勘校，修正和潤色，但一定會有諸多不盡人意的地方，敬請學者方家不吝賜教。在此筆者向以下諸位譯者

致以最誠摯的感謝與敬意：費正華博士（Jennifer Feeley），笑川先生
（Matt Turner），翁海瑩女士，香港大學中文系的柯夏智教授（Lucas
Klein），美國國家大學的戴邁河教授（Michael M. Day），東北大學外
國語學院的馮溢教授。另外，陸敬思教授（Chris Lupke），楊小濱博
士，宋明煒教授，翟月琴教授，Martin Winter先生，Ellen Zweig女士以
及我的英文系同事 Ellen Friedman和Michael Robertson教授等諸位朋友
也對本部詩集提供了重要的幫助，筆者在此向他們致以由衷的謝意。

　　筆者在此萬分感謝旅美畫家楊識宏大師慷慨解囊，同意將其優美
作品《空山靈雨》用作本詩集封面；也萬分感謝臺灣書法家李默父先
生為本詩集題寫了蒼勁有力的書名，他們二位的大作均完美契合了筆
者的詩意幻象，一定使本詩集增輝萬分。

　　感謝秀威資訊的鄭伊庭主任將拙作納入出版計畫，使這些歷經久
遠的文字能有機會拂去灰塵，見諸於世。徐佑驊小姐對文稿進行了精
心的編輯與細查，筆者深表謝意。

　　最後，在筆者三十七年修行「深呼吸」中，每時每刻都與全家
人息息相通，時刻得到他們的呵護，摯愛與支持，尤其是內子盧丹跟
隨筆者跋山涉水，共同呼吸生命的真氣，愛子米稻，愛女米顆給予了
筆者無窮的人生樂趣與鼓勵，他們的愛護關懷始終是筆者繼續「深呼
吸」的精神支柱和力量源泉。謹將這本微不足道的詩集獻給他們。

米家路
2018年10月10日
於新澤西普林斯頓

Editorial Notes and Acknowledgments

The poems collected in this volume were written during the past thirty-seven years of my literary pursuit. Most of the poems are presented to readers for the first time. This volume is divided into three parts in reverse chronological order. First part titled "Verses from the Sky's Edge" includes the poems I wrote between the years of 1996 and 2018 when I crossed the Pacific Ocean to study for my doctoral degree at the University of California at Davis and then began working at The College of New Jersey. Second part titled "Cloud Divination at Mount Gele" includes the poems I wrote between the years of 1985-1995 when I finished college and started to teach, then went to Beijing University to study for my MA degree in Comparative Literature, and then moved to study at CUHK. Third part titled "Flashes of Youth" includes the poems I wrote during my undergraduate studies at SISU between 1981 and 1984.

Publishing a Chinese-English bilingual edition of my poems is a daunting task. I am so lucky to have entrusted my poems to the hands of excellent English translators. I can't sufficiently express my gratitude to the following translators who have given their valuable time to translate my poems from Chinese into English in such a short time: Jennifer Feeley, Matt Turner and his wife Haiying Weng, Lucas Klein from the University of Hong Kong, Michael M. Day from National University in San Diego, CA, and Feng Yi from Northeast University in China. I am also grateful to Michael Robertson, Ellen Friedman, Rob Wilson, Chris Lupke, Yang Xiaobin, Song Mingwei, Zhai Yueqin, Martin Winter, and Ellen Zweig who have offered their valuable suggestions for revision of the manuscripts.

I am especially grateful for master painter Chihung Yang who generously gave his permission for me to use his painting "Soul Rains in the Empty Mountain" for the cover of my book. I also thank calligrapher Li Mofu for writing the most beautiful title for my book.

Lastly and above all, my deepest thanks go to my wife Lucy Lu, my son Dao Mi and my daughter Coco Mi, for their unreserved spiritual support throughout these years of my literary pursuits. It is to them that this humble volume is dedicated.

Mi Jialu
October 10, 2018
Princeton, NJ

新詩集題記

　　　　　　　仿　威廉・卡洛斯・威廉斯《紅色手推車》

那麼多
依賴

一團藍色的
呼吸

迸發繁星
銀花

旁邊是一個
空籃子

　　　　　　　　　　　2018.3.1於普林斯頓

New Poetry Book

After William Carlos Williams' *"The Red Wheelbarrow"*

So much depends
upon

a blue puff
air

radiated with starry
sparks

beside an empty
basket.

March 1, 2018. Princeton

目　次

輯二 望氣歌樂山（1985-1995）
Cloud Divination on Mount Gele

輯三 青春流光（1981-1984）
Flashes of Youth

天涯離騷

1996-2018

Verses from the Sky's Edge

望雪

春分時節
大雪卻悄然而至
落滿了後院

困攔在室內
望著窗外的雪花
瞥見一隻孤鳥竄起
突然想到雪意的滋味

比如
背靠火爐
透過明亮的玻璃
觀看外面的飛雪
與
佇立在飛雪中
受撲面雪花的拍打
有什麼根本的不同

我猜想
透過玻璃觀雪
玻璃更冷
心更暖和
望雪其實是望月
就是對空白的遙望

Glancing at Snow

The time of spring equinox
Yet a heavy snow quietly arrives
filling the backyard

Idling inside the house
Watching snowflakes outside the window
I glimpse a solitary bird scurrying about
and suddenly a taste of snow comes to mind

For instance
Having my back against a fireplace
peering through bright glass
at snow flying outside
and
Standing amid the falling snow
flakes fluttering on my face
What is the fundamental difference between them

I suppose
Observing snow through glass
the colder the glass
the warmer the heart
To watch snow is really to look at the moon
a distant gaze upon a blank space

佇立飛雪中觀雪
心更冷
雪更暖和
望雪其實是望水
就是對逝者的凝視

透過玻璃望雪
月是一種不可捉摸的幻影
佇立雪中嚼雪
雪花漫過舌頭便成了血脈

2018.3.21於普林斯頓

Standing in snow watching it fluttering
the colder the heart
the warmer the snow
To watch snow is really to look at water
a constant gaze upon the departed

Watching snow through glass
the moon is an ungraspable illusion
Chewing snow while standing in it
the flakes that soak through the tongue become blood

March 21, 2018. Princeton, NJ
(English Trans. Michael Day)

春日響雷

驚蟄的濕氣
鬆動泥土
草根之下
幼蟲翻動腰身
細嫩的觸鬚
接通光的暖流
巢穴中的黑暗肺葉
瞬間扇動血紅的翅膀

宇宙的至高祕密
隨陣陣炸雷
自天而降
從蓓蕾初綻的蕊口
豁然開啟

2018.3.8於普林斯頓

Thunder of Spring

The damp air of Waking-Insects season
stirs up the soil
and beneath grass roots
larvae stir and stretch
tender antennae
connecting with the warm stream of light
In the nest, the black lobes of lungs
instantly flap their blood-red wings

The supreme secret of the universe
follows each clap of thunder
down from the sky
from a bud's early burst of a pistil
flashes wide open

March 8, 2018. Princeton, NJ
(English Trans. Michael Day)

雪中迷蝶

我為何來此？
背鄉離井，朝
更死亡的方向逼近
別了吧，暖春啊，暖春

何以如此殘暴，兇狠？
持續向下的伏擊，將
我的羽翼散亂，撲騰
狂醉的氣流激起浪漫

誰的夢將我喚醒？
戴面具的影子懸空，赤裸
揮動旌旗，拍擊渾圓的日鼓
那鼓聲令我顫慄，耳葉紛墜

多麼想跳一曲更刺骨的花舞哦
百合花瓣瓣赴死的捲揚，旋滑
令這撕裂的愛情更淒美
我柔軟的翼啊，會斑斕在下個春日？

2010.12.8於普林斯頓

Butterfly in Snow

Why have I come here?
Far from home, toward
a deader destiny
So long, spring, my warm spring

Why such violence, such brutality?
The ambush continues downward, scattering
my wings, thumping
Ecstatic airflows arouse romance

Whose dream will wake me?
A masked shadow perched high, naked
waving a flag, striking a round sun drum
that shakes my trunk, ears falling like leaves

How I long for a chilling flower dance
A whirlwind of dying lily petals, sliding
bringing this torn love a sadder beauty
By next spring will my soft wings be resplendent?

December 8, 2010. Princeton
(English Trans. Lucas Klein)

行刑隊進行曲（截句）

1

集結號奏響：嗚啦啦，嗚啦啦
立正，一，二，三，向左看齊
預備，上膛，放：砰砰，噠噠

2

劈啪，劈啪啪，劈劈啪啪
腦袋炸裂，迸開如映山紅
血漿奔流如注，嘩啦啦

3

稍息，稍息，齊步走，嗖嗖嗖
長長的舌頭呼哧呼哧撲騰而出
舔，吮，啄著血漿如乳液

4

舔不淨爆裂的淤血，忽而嚎叫
群狼撕碎骨頭，猛爪向天
月食劃過，宇宙僅露出猙獰的眼

5

行刑隊連夜急行軍，為了
將死亡傳遞給黎明，在向太陽
揚頭之前給日葵致命一擊

The Firing Squad March (Segments)

1

The assembly's call resounds: *wu lala, wu lala*
Attention! One, two, three. Aim left!
Load, ready, fire: *pow pow, rat tat*

2

Cr-crack, cr-cr-crack, cr-cr-crack-ack
Head splits open, bursting like an azalea
Blood gushing, *hua lala*

3

At ease, at ease. Together, *whoosh*
Long tongues flop out panting
Pecking, sucking, lapping at the blood like milk

4

Congested blood can't be licked clean, suddenly screaming
A wolf pack rips the bones, clawing to the sky
The lunar eclipse slides by, the cosmos showing its savage eyes

5

The firing squad is on the march even at night, so as to
deliver death to dawn, a coup de grace to the sunflower
before it can raise its face to the sun

6

行刑隊的刺刀寒光閃亮，插進雪中
更白，從鮮肉中抽出更紅
滴血的刃上照出烏鴉垂涎的喙

7

行刑隊的最高美學：目──空──無──人
唯從最高統帥的指令：子彈的速度
扳機一放，空氣就彈出死亡的硝煙

8

行刑隊在麥場練靶，掃蕩炯炯麥芒
打麥，打麥，碎麥成餅，獻祭眾生
打麥，打麥，麥粒入土，春來萌芽

9

七月流火，行刑隊截肢，套上假手
面具隨骷髏旗翻轉，玻璃眼球瞄準
五星銀彈傾瀉，射向一把空空的椅子

10

從今以後，面對行刑隊
良眾合力搬動空椅，安放於海濱
面朝大海，佇候從浪中歸來的淘金人

2017.7.27-28於普林斯頓

6

The bayonets of the firing squad glimmer in the cold light, stuck into snow
whiter they turn, but a deeper red when pulled out of fresh flesh
Drooling crow beaks reflect in blades dripping with blood

7

The highest aesthetic of the firing squad: *no – one – in – sight*
They follow only the highest commander's decree: pull the trigger
at bullet speed, and the air will jolt from death's gunpowder smoke

8

The firing squad practices shooting on the threshing ground,
    sweeping awns of wheat
Thresh wheat, thresh wheat, make its innards into cakes, to be
    sacrificed to all the living
Thresh wheat, thresh wheat, send its seeds into the soil, to sprout
    again next spring

9

Burning hot in July, the firing squad had amputations, putting on prosthetic hands
Masks revolved like jolly roger flags, and glass eyes took their aim
Five-star silver bullets rained down, shooting at an empty chair

10

Henceforth, when facing the firing squad
Good people join forces, moving the empty chair to the seaside
And face the ocean, waiting for the gold digger to return from the waves

July 27-28, 2017. Princeton
(English Trans. Lucas Klein)

暴風雪襲來之前觀鳥

早春，霜寒
雪意嗖嗖，枯枝泛綠
藍喜鵲覓食，心悅

頭往上望，晴空萬里
低頭下視，嫩草濕潤
中空翻動著興奮的彩羽

日子就這樣隨意，安然
不料明日暴風雪咋起
何處是家？何日再相聚？

　　　　　　　　　　　　　2017.3.13於普林斯頓

Watching Birds Before a Blizzard

An early spring, a frosty cold
A swirling sense of snow, bare branches suffusing green
A bluejay is hunting food, a happy heart

A gaze aloft, a thousand miles of blue sky
A look below, baby grass moist
and in mid-air is ruffling with fluttering colorful feathers

The days pass freely like this, so peaceful
Alas！Who knows tomorrow brings a blizzard
Where the home lies, what day we'll meet again?

March 13, 2017. Princeton
(English Trans. Michael Day)

秋日的草垛

節氣的烏鴉，來回
盤旋於乾草垛之上
發出的嘶鳴，令空氣
愈加乾燥，耳鼓如潮

偽裝的田園景色
令收穫愈加疲憊
遊人散漫的目光
漏掉了不規則的幻美

2017.8.15於普林斯頓

Haystacks in Autumn

Autumnal crows, to and fro
circling over haystacks
crying out, making the air
even drier, eardrums roar like floods

A pastoral scene in disguise
makes harvest even more exhausting
The careless gaze of tourists
leaves out irregular illusive beauty

August 15, 2017. Princeton
(English Trans. Michael Day)

致青春

那青春抗議的熾焰，
曾無懼地燃燒。

那些扔向鋼盔的石頭，
彈回來，擊碎我們心臟。

那些傷痕累累的旗手，倒下，
昂揚的唯有那眼赤紅的瞳孔。

我們年少的風暴騎手啊，展翅，
一撒把馳過被劫持的深淵。

2017.5.4於普林斯頓

To Youth

The flames that ignited the protests of youth,
once fearlessly blazed.

The rocks that were thrown at steel helmets,
bounced back, shattering our hearts.

The scar-ridden standard-bearers fell down,
and all that remained uplifted was their eyes' crimson pupils.

Ah, the storm riders of our youth, spread your wings,
cast off from the abducted abyss with one daring leap.

May 4, 2017. Princeton
(English Trans. Michael Day)

麋鹿

蹄聲踏出江南，隨洋流
遷徙英倫，如鬥星轉移
神父的紅棕披風翻飛，那蹄聲
又踏回濕潤的江南，靈角呼啦
穿越風風雨雨的一百年

2018.1.26於普林斯頓

Elaphures

Hoofbeats step out of the Southern land, follow oceanic streams
migrating to England, like a shifting Dipper
Priest's cardinal red cloak whipping on the wind, the hoofbeats
tread again in the humid Southern Yangtze River, their horns howl
passing through the wind and the rain of a hundred years

January 26, 2018. Princeton
(English Trans. Michael Day)

早茶

清新而又充沛，如綠茶
舒卷，從高山的霧氣
吐露雨水的甘甜，
醒過黑夜的困頓，
滋潤凡人的心間。

醒茶面向晨光，
玻璃杯頓生暖流，
茶葉千回百轉，
光合的輻射，催生
又一次輪迴轉世。

2018.1.25於普林斯頓

Morning Tea

Refreshing and vigorous, green tea
is rolling out, from a high mountain mist
spitting out the sweetness of rain water,
removing the weariness of a black night,
moistening a commoner's mind.

Awakening tea looks to the morning light,
the glass instantly emits a warm current,
as tea leaves endlessly twist and turn ,
a photosynthetic radiation brings to life
yet another cycle of rebirth.

January 25, 2018. Princeton
(English Trans. Michael Day)

裂

二月某日清晨驅車路上，
偶然瞥見一棵大樹從中劈開，
其扭曲的斷枝弧形般聳立
在積雪的大地上，裂變的
曲折美令人詫異。

　　　　裂
　　　　　裂
　　　　　　裂
　　裂　　　　　裂
　　　　　裂
　　　　　裂
　　　　　裂

從垂直的向度，以勢不可擋的
渴望，撕裂皮和肉
毫不畏懼墜落，向下，向下
朝崇高反向剝離
——裂必是一種低度的誕生

掙脫軀幹的瞬間

Split

(Driving early one February morning,

I glimpsed a large tree split open,

its broken branches twisted into a towering arch

on land covered by a mantle of snow, the fissile

twisted beauty astonished me.)

S
P
L
I
T
Split   Split
S
P
L
I
T

In a vertical direction, an unstoppable

desire lacerates skin and flesh

fearlessly dropping, downwards, down

peeling away against the sublime

————A split must be a lower form of birth

The instant of breaking free of the trunk

緣於地心的暴力，扭曲
釋放刻骨銘心的痛，聳立的
糾纏塑造生動的大地
——裂必然呈示大道的生成

誰曾瞥見這劇變的時辰?
它或許發生在天地混沌的暗夜
或許發生在天地開啟的黎明
以弧弦的姿勢，持續彎曲
直至意志力在零點折斷

裂的碎聲從何處濺出
是從軀體內的筋絡處
還是從騷動的根莖處？
涅槃的葉片嗖嗖拍擊
斷枝間懸空的積雪

裂必是一個純然的動詞
它不及物的開放溶解塵土，撩撥
腐爛的氣息，令折翅的
羽毛自由下墜，真空無限的輕
水銀般彌漫，擦亮一束束光芒

2015.2.10於普林斯頓

pulled by the violent force of gravity, the twisting

releases an unforgettable pain, the towering

tangle shapes a lively earth

———A split must reveal the becoming of the Great Way

Who has glimpsed the time of this great upheaval

It might have transpired at night when heaven and earth are muddled

or at the dawn when heaven and earth are opened up

in the posture of an arc, continuously bending

up until will power snaps off at the zero point

From where does the crack of the split splatter out

from the veins of the body

or from convulsive rootstock?

Leaves released from Nirvana swish and rustle over

the snow accumulated in midair in the broken branches

Split must be an unmitigated action word

It opens intransitively, dissolving the dust, provoking

an odor of decay, causing fractured

feathers to fall freely, the limitless lightness of the void

spreading out like quicksilver, polishing ray after ray of light

Febraury 10, 2015. Princeton
(English Trans. Michael Day)

恆河上的心經

恆河之水自何處來？
——自雪峰深處，佛說
如何而來？
——自由流淌，佛說
流向何處？
——流向低處，佛說

客想過河不？大宗師問
不過，客答
為何不過？大宗師問
過了此岸還得回來，客答
何解？大宗師問
此刻就在彼岸，客答

客／大宗師：菠蘿蜜多，菠蘿蜜多

恆河上昨夜有大乘擱淺
喜馬拉雅山冰川雪峰遁失
————————CNN報導
祝賀雅魯藏布江截流成功
世界最高大壩將屹立雄偉高原
————————CCTV報導

恆河之水自何處而來？
——自空處而來，佛說

Heart Sutra on the Ganges River

Where does the water in the Ganges come from?
——From deep snow, spoke the Buddha
By how does it come?
——Freely flowing, spoke the Buddha
To where does it flow?
——All the way down, thus spoke the Buddha

Want to cross the river? Asked the Guru
No, the traveler answered
Why not? Asked the Guru
Still coming back after crossing, the traveler answered
In what sense? Asked the Guru
We are now on the other shore, the traveler answered

Traveler/Guru: Prajñpramit, Prajñpramit!

A big boat was stranded on the Ganges last night
Snow peaks on Himalayan glaciers fled
——————————CNN reported
Congratulations on stopping the Brahmaputra River
The world's highest dam stands on majestic plateau
——————————CCTV reported

Where does the water in the Ganges come from?
——From the emptiness, spoke the Buddha

如何而來？
──擺渡者的竹竿，佛說
流向何處？
──色即空，空即色，佛說

2010.5.13於普林斯頓

By what means?

——By the ferryman's bamboo pole, spoke the Buddha

To where does it flow?

——Form is emptiness, and emptiness is form, spoke the Buddha

May 13, 2010. Princeton
(English Trans. Lucas Klein)

夢遊者與貓

子夜，節氣的鐘擺潮濕，
當報時者輕敲大地，
一剎幽光閃爍，照亮，
夢遊人瘦削的坐騎。

如水銀般流瀉，
奪命的眼神追逐暈月，
夢遊人點燃渡河的青燈。

星夜兼程啊，碎步依依，
踐踏睡眠，彗星的羽翼。

銀河裡槳櫓散亂，蒙面俠
行走於鍍金的水面，
打撈黎明前的鮮魚。

行者正隨霧氣摩挲，
松花繽紛，激動的雙掌，
撲哧，從黑暗出發，
信使的令箭穿越隧道，
擊中銅鏡，甲骨閃裂：

A Sleepwalker and a Cat

Midnight, the solar pendulum swings damp,
When night watchman softly knocks on the earth,
a dusky light flickers, lights up
the gaunt mount of the sleepwalker.

Drifting like quicksilver,
his lethal look chases a halo moon,
The sleepwalker lights a lamp before crossing the river.

Hurry in the starry night, yet his steps keep jolting,
wings of a comet trample on the hours of his sleep.

In the Milky Way, scatter sculls, a masked knight
walks on the surface of gilded water,
hauling up fresh fish at predawn.

The walker moves with caresses of the mist,
Pine pollen riotous, his palms agitated,
Phuuusss, shooting out from darkness,
the messenger's arrow flies through the tunnel,
striking a bronze mirror, shells and bones instantly crack:

「嘿，夢遊人，
時間不早了，上路吧，
免費送您一程，
過河後別回頭，
一路保重!」

　　　　　　　　　　　　　　2010.5.24於普林斯頓

"Hey, sleepwalker,
Time is running out, let's hit the road,
I'll give you a free ride,
Don't look back after crossing the river,
and take care along the way!"

May 24, 2010. Princeton
(English Trans. Michael Day)

立夏偶感

五月的向晚，立夏第二日
火舌般的風撩撥花粉
竄突的觸鬚令呼吸暴動
陽臺上，四隻幼貓撲騰空氣
拂拭過敏中的微微醉意

如發酵的酒窖，街頭爵士樂
彌漫，行人跌跌撞撞
忙於追逐白日的幻影
紅松鼠清掃巢穴，松果
倒立，預卜全球的溫室效應

在一塊青石條上，眼神端坐
柳絮當空紛揚，迷朦遠景
天女奇妙的花籃倒空春色
也倒空青春期的躁動

殘忍，如綠葉的刀片
從蓓蕾的深處，開裂
天地的果實：海底耶無限的妖冶

2010.5.20於普林斯頓

Impromptu at the Start of Summer

A dusk in May, the second day of summer
A wind like tongue of fire whips up the pollen
A sudden scurry of cirrus throbs breathing
On the sundeck, four kittens flop about in the air
whisk away the faint dizziness of allergies

Like a fermenting wine cellar, street jazz
fills the air, pedestrians stagger about
busy chasing mirages of daylight
A red squirrel cleans out its nest, pinecones
upside down, foretelling global greenhouse effect

A glance lingers above a strip of limestone
Catkins flutter through the air, blurring distant prospects
Fairy's wondrous basket of flowers empties itself of spring
also empties out the delirium of adolescence

Cruelty, like the razor of a green leaf
from flower's innermost bud, splits open
fruit of the universe : a boundless voluptuousness of coco de mer

May 20, 2010. Princeton
(English Trans. Michael Day)

米蘭詩篇

或
幻想米蘭的十三種方式

一

四月，潮濕的空氣彌漫，
水花在夢中穿行，濺迸，
米蘭盛開的花朵沿向陽坡
搖曳，多彩斑斕。

米蘭啊！你的容顏如此秘不可測。

二

午後，一匹東方的飛毯
在氤氳的天空舒卷，
如閃亮的綢緞，輕盈而至，
渴望之門欣然洞開。

米蘭啊！你的肌膚光亮柔媚。

三

看哪！棕櫚樹在瘋狂擺動，
如風的激情灌滿簇葉，
驚醒長夜裡酣睡的戀人，夏日
在新雨的街口處，恭候伊人的歸程。

Milan Cantos

or

Thirteen Ways of Fantasizing about Milan

1

April, suffused with humid air,

Water splashes spread through dreams, splattering,

As the flowers that blossom in Milan on the sunny hill

sway, glimmer with multicolors.

Milan, how unfathomable is your face!

2

Afternoon, an Oriental flying carpet

rolled up in the enshrouding sky

Like a flash of brocade, lissome in its arrival,

The gates of longing are flung open with joy.

Milan, your skin is soft and smooth!

3

Look! The palms sway wildly,

As if their fronds were filled with passion's winds,

Startling the slumbering lovers in the night, summer

At a recently rained street corner, where I await her return.

米蘭啊！你的雲裳迢遙旖旎。

四

採茶人在青山上勞作，
山泉之水喚醒農耕好時節，
清苦的路途隨風延展，
青茶蕩漾，山客擊鼓吟唱，

米蘭啊！你可聞到那迷幻的幽香？

五

勇敢的水手築舟踏浪遠遊，
他夢想的樂園懸在天際，
新月當空，水手吹起了竹笛，
海面上浮起他無言的孤寂，

米蘭啊！你可知海底椰迷惑的妖豔？

六

海藻在潮汐中瘋狂舞蹈，
群魚在選擇棲居的命運，
海嘯夜襲大地，候鳥
葡伏在黑色的岩石上，占卦，

米蘭啊！你可聽見水手搏擊的呼喚？

Milan, your cloud cover is distant but enchanting!

4

The tea-picker labors on the green hill,

Springwater waking farming's good season,

A rough road stretching with the wind,

As the tea ripples, the mountain men drumming and chanting,

Milan, do you smell that hallucinatory aroma?

5

The brave sailor crafts a boat to travel afar onto the waves,

Dreaming of a paradise hanging from the sky,

and a new moon in the sky, the sailor plays a bamboo flute,

His wordless solitude floating on the sea,

Milan, do you know the perplexing demon of the coco de mer?

6

In the tide seaweed dances in trance,

Fish choose their dwelling fate,

A tsunami hits land at night, and migrating birds

lean over the black volcanic rock, consulting oracles,

Milan, can you hear the call of the sailor's struggle?

七

水手臨瀑布潑墨，手掌向上，
他的拋灑浪漫，欣昂，
畫布坦裸，抒情的扭曲，
癲狂如搖櫓，劃出浪濤和妄想，

米蘭啊！你可遠眺那鼓動的紅帆？

八

雲翳在天上暴動，它殘酷的黑色
吞噬運河，善良的公民們在岸上
點燈，恐懼驅逐恐懼，期待閃電
撲救遁入深淵裡的落日，火舌的臉譜，

米蘭啊！那船是否駛向更兇猛的地平線？

九

野心，如水中的流雲，甜美，
與水手一見鍾情，更傷感，
運河易脆的甬道，給孤獨
致命一擊，晶體碎裂於背叛，

米蘭啊！那火焰可焚燒你詭異的面具？

十

琴聲奏響，緋紅的柿子透露祕密，
季風擊鼓，地中海的蔚藍翻卷，

7

Approaching the waterfall the sailor spills ink, palms up,

His spill is romantic, exalted,

But the canvas is bare, a lyrical twist,

Mad like a scull, rowing out of waves and wishful thinking,

Milan, can you spot the agitated red sail?

8

The nebula riot in the skies, their brutal blackness

swallowes the canal, while nice citizens on the shore

light lanterns, fear driving out fear, waiting for lightning

to extinguish the sun setting into the abyss, masks of tongues of fire,

Milan, is that boat coursing to a more violent horizon?

9

Ambition, like clouds drifting in water, luscious,

in love with the sailor at first sight, more sentimental,

The canal's fragile passageway, a coup de grace

for solitude, crystal cracking under betrayal,

Milan, will the flames burn up your bizarre mask?

10

The zither resounds, scarlet persimmons divulge their secrets,

The monsoon beats its drum, the blue of the Mediterranean roiling,

點染蝴蝶的彩翼，氣流暈眩，
憤怒的水手刺擊女巫千年的符咒，

米蘭啊！你光陰的玫瑰可否綻放如葵？

十一

多少人遠道而來瞻仰你碩大的空地，
虛空盛裝天使的糧食？為何朝聖者
向飢餓開戰？頹敗的石頭呢喃，上帝
感傷的慈悲，都摩如盲人撫摸潦倒的裸體，

米蘭啊！那鴿子閃亮的瞳孔可瞥見失魂的夜歸人？

十二

山體洞開，一條柔軟的天梯譁然而下，
阿爾卑斯山的雪花逃竄，隱逸於平原的梨花林，
石砌的街道潤濕，梭子朝拜旋轉的圖案，
教堂天窗上的彩葉被火柴嘎然擦亮，

米蘭啊！你暗河的冰水可否滋潤陌生人乾裂的嘴唇？

十三

米蘭並非花，天堂鳥也並非一隻鳥，
這含混的命名令我亢奮又攪擾，米蘭城裡
應該有米蘭花吧？天堂鳥中也有鳥吧？
如果皆無，以我這詩篇幻作花，也作鳥，

dyeing butterfly wings, vertigo in airflow,

The angry sailor thrusts a witch's thousand-year curses,

Milan, will the rose of your time burst in bloom?

11

How many have come from afar to revere your vast spaces,

The void holds the angels' grain? Why do pilgrims

make war on hunger? Crumbling stones murmur, God's

sentimental mercy, Duomo being stroked like blind, impoverished nudity,

Milan, will the dove's shimmering pupil spot the lost soul returning at night?

12

The cave in the mountain opens, the soft ladder of heaven crashes down,

Snow flees on the Alps, retreating into pear blossom groves on the plains,

Stone step streets soaked, loom shuttles prostrating to gyrating patterns,

Colored leaves on cathedral stained glass were suddenly lighted by matches,

Milan, will the ice water of your dark rivers irrigate a stranger's chapped lips?

13

Milan is not a flower, nor are birds of paradise birds,

These ambiguities of naming both excite and annoy me, in the city of Milan

Should there be milan flowers? Birds in birds of paradise?

If all is nothing, then may my poem be a flower, and a bird,

米蘭啊！請傾聽吧，一個人在思念另一座城市的人，
我可否獻上這詩篇，懸在桅杆上引導死海上的迷路人？

2009.4-6紐約-芝加哥-普林斯頓

Milan, listen to me, a person is longing for a person of another city!

Can I dedicate my poem by hanging it on a mast to guide the lost on the Dead Sea?

April-June, 2009. New York – Chicago – Princeton
(English Trans. Lucas Klein)

異鄉人的秋日

之一

秋風吹起來
刮出時間的灰塵
落日的背景下
群鴉欣然舞蹈

夜色中閃躲的眼睛
搜尋青春的滑動
動物遊弋的身姿
擴展我們無限的遐想

田野，穀物昂然
鐮刀在飛舞　慶典

之二

秋日緩行
山頂上萬頃雲田
莊稼細語潺潺
花狗沿山徑竄行
草叢一群斑鳥騰起

秋景無限迷朦
消隱的一些植物
在深情地回眸

Autumn for the Stranger

1

The autumn wind blows
Kicking up the dust of time
Under the background of the sunset
the crows dance with joy

Evasive eyes in the night
search for the sliding of youth
The cruising gait of the animals
expands our boundless reveries

In the field, grain is upright
The sickle flies, a celebration

2

The time of autumn moves slowly
The vast cloud field expands on the mountaintop
Crops sway in whispers
The spotted dog scurries along the mountain path
A flock of birds leap from the bushes

The autumn scene is boundlessly hazy
Some vanished plants
glance back lovingly

山坳上的風口
螢火蟲在演奏
無聲的交響曲

之三

秋日的餘暉
一定照在銅鏡之中
鋥亮的溫暖
十指也無法觸入

唯有水鄉的竹笛
在彌漫的江波上
捕捉潛流的誘惑
但卵石的擊出
便搗碎了光的幻美

啊啊，那悠然遠去的
是我們蝶翼般的風帆

之四

秋日少年遠行
出發前預備：
夢的擔子
空的地圖

軌道直奔遠方
路途遙遙
少年的夢想

to the wind gap over the col
Fireflies perform
a soundless symphony

3

An autumn sunset glow
will shine into the bronze mirror
A shimmering warmth
can't even be absorbed by ten fingers

Only a bamboo flute from a river town
resounds over ripples
hunting for the undercurrent's seduction
But the strike of a pebble
shatters the illusoriness of light

Ah, all that has departed so leisurely
Is our butterfly wing-like sail

4

In Autumn,　a youth travels afar
Pre-departure preparations:
Dream's load
An empty map

The track runs into the distance
The road is distant
Youthful dreams

點擊濕的傷心

手指伸入天際
雲朵白棉般擁抱
有些輕浮的愛情
沉浸於痛的空間

捲揚的運動
使少年在遠方失蹤

之五

我用竹葉丈量日影
書與書之間是詞語行距
搖擺的青竹
影子歪斜直下
命脈高漲

葉片滑行
邊緣蠕動的汁液
令激情無法迷失
令信念砰然開放
鐘擺上下的空間

正是日影虛度
生命無情的顫慄

double-click a wet heartache

Fingers reach into the sky
Clouds hug like white cottons
Some frivolous loves
immerse in the space of pain

The movement of the whirlwind
makes the youth disappear in the distance

5

I measure shadows of the sun with bamboo leaves
Between books is the line spacing of words
Swinging green bamboo
Shadows slant downward
The lifeline at high tide

Leaves slide
Juices creeping on the edges
make the passion unable to get lost
make belief thud open
The space that pendulum swings up and down

is the solar shadow slipping by
life's merciless shudder

之六

秋日還鄉
煙草之味潛行
土壤脫開空殼
生長一片自由

鹽味之水
思想纏繞之神祕
偉大之手也枯萎
桑葚沿稻田滑行

夢的尖刀之上
是秋日燃燒後
群蟻仰望的繁星
和那空寂的鄉愁

之七

秋日落葉蕭蕭
少年立步出關
將艾葉編織
在頭頂的斗笠中

風吹拂黃沙
無限的廣漠
彌漫醉人的薰香
少年目極遠方

6

On the way back home in autumn
The scent of tobacco slithers
As soil casts out shells
growth is a kind of freedom

Water that emits the flavor of salt
Mysteries of tangling thoughts
The noble hands are also withering
Mulberries walk alongside rice paddies

Above the knife's edge of a dream
Is the time after autumn's burning
The constellations that an army of ants looks up
and the solitary homesickness

7

Autumn leaves rustle
The youth rises to cross the border
Weaving mugwort leaves
in the top bamboo hat

The wind blows yellow sands
The limitless desert
Inundated with an intoxicating sweet scent
The youth looks off to the distance

彷彿有一匹駿馬奔來
塵土蔓延無際
少年端坐於枯木之下
鳥翼之上啟明星冉冉升起

之八

秋風中的愛情
是影子撫摸影子
溫暖之外是眺望
一段道路的寓意

有無蔚藍的海水
追逐夢遊上岸的魚
離奇般的等候
岸與岸的距離

命運的潮聲
是否隱藏最高真理
誰將來撫摸
波光消失的一剎那

之九

在秋日的哈德遜河邊
火車逆流而行
滔滔景色卷起
遊人悠遠的瞭望

As if a steed at gallop
Dust extends to the infinite
The young man sits under a dead tree
Venus rises on a bird wing

8

Love in autumn wind
Is shadow stroking shadow
Beyond warmth is overlook
The trope of a road

Whether there is blue seawater
Chasing fish that sleepwalk ashore
A bizarre waiting
The distance shore to shore

The tide sound of destiny
Is whether to cover up the highest truth
Who will caress
the split-second of waves'vanishing gleaming

9

Autumn on the Hudson River
The train goes backwards
Surging scenery rolls up
the distant gaze of travelers

岸邊的殘堡閃掠
群鳥嘩啦飛揚
移民者開墾疆土
原著民流離他鄉

黛色的山巒
被殘陽籠罩
迸火的車輪輾出
異鄉人的憂傷

之十

隨簇擁的人群
捲入廣場的渦流
旋動的光束和泡沫
浸泡文明的偽善

彷彿時間嘎然停轉
人群在嘈雜的喧譁中
紛紛奪路而逃竄
猙獰的面孔撒滿街頭

淪陷已久的雙塔
如兩條失敗的鯨魚
注視權力與意志的廢墟
大西洋上的巨輪，鳴笛
宣告航標燈逃逸的征程

Ruined castles flash by the bank
A flock of birds whoosh up
The immigrants reclaim the frontier
and Native Americans roam homeless

Dark green mountain ranges
are enshrouded by the setting sun
Fire-spitting wheels unroll
the sadness of strangers

10

Following the clusters of people
Coiled into the vortex of the square
Rotating at the speed of light and foam
that soaks civilization's hypocrisies

As if time has screeched still
The crowd in a melee of noise
clamor for the road to flee
Ferocious faces scattering over the streets

Fallen Twin Towers
Like two defeated whales
stare at the ruins of power and will
The giant ships on the Atlantic whistle
Proclaiming the routes of beacon's escape

之十一

秋色是否需要描述
直觀的凝視
呈現果實溫暖的旖旎
而隱喻的詭詐
逾越豔陽曝裸的倦意

詩人的野心
行走在無光的海域
打撈失落久遠的輪迴
命運的風信子
追逐星光幽暗的幻影

豁然回首，秋色的寓意
則是大地滌蕩之後
裸露出的林中空茫

之十二

秋雨淅瀝而下
節氣在泥濘中
詭秘潛行，落葉
腐爛於塵土

一些歷史的想像
似曾相似，日復一日
在塵埃的道路上翻滾
抒情的濃墨潑灑渡頭

11

Does sense of autumn need to be described
Can a gaze by intuition
present fruit's warm charm
Or a metaphor's trickery
transcend the sun's denuded weariness

The poet's ambition
traverses in a sunless sea
Salvaging long-lost samsara
The hyacinth of fate
chases starlight's gloomy specters

Flashing back, the moral of autumn
After the wash-away of the earth
will expose the clearing in the woods

12

Autumn rain gushes down
Solar terms fall in the mud
Sneaking secretly, fallen leaves
are rotting in dust

Some historical imaginations
appear déjà vu, day after day
Tumbled on the roads of dirt
Lyrical ink spilling over the ferry crossing

聲音依稀傳來
碎雨點化故事
今朝的人物和事蹟
傳頌於大地春秋

之十三

帝國的秋日
易開罐廢棄
人民依然焦渴
高聳入雲的黑煙
席捲GDP沉灰的天空

在通往地球的咽喉處
人民呼吸的鼻息淹沒

帝國的群馬狂奔
人民的莊稼被收割
不可啜飲的污水
揮霍魚兒愛情的歡愉

在帝國蒼茫的宮殿裡
失敗的旗幟飄揚
骰子弧線般拋擊，尖叫
廣場上向日葵狼狽而逃

之十四

又臨十一月，冬霜
悲秋如稻草人

Voices come faintly
Broken rain triggers stories
Today's talents and deeds
spread spring and autumn over the earth

13

An empire in autumn
Tin-can wastage
People are still thirsty
Towering black smoke
rolls up a GDP-grey sky

Passing through the throat of the earth
The breath of the people was choked

The empire's horses gallop forth
Crops of the people were harvested
Undrinkable wastewater
squanders the joyous love of fish

In the empire's vast palaces
Wave flags of failure
Dice tossed in an arc, screaming
Sunflowers flee the square

14

Another November comes, winter frost
Autumn sad as a scarecrow

在空地上佇立
驚恐獵物的缺失

蒙面人持長矛而來
對峙，醉漢般舞蹈
面具生火，點燃
頹敗的玉米迷宮

蔬菜嫵媚地招搖
暗示一年舒卷的收成
建在大道上的糧倉
貯存遠遊人的胸臆

秋去冬至的這個時辰
帝國又硝煙彌漫
祖國也沙塵滾滾
詩人啊，詩人
往世界綠色掌心去朝聖吧

2007.10.11於普林斯頓

stands in an open space
was shocked at the prey lost

A masked man arrives with a spear
Facing off, dancing like a drunkard
On fire, the mask lights
a crumbling corn maze

Vegetables sway with charm
Implying a year of leisurely harvest
The granary built on the broad road
Stores dreams of distant travelers

At the time when autumn goes at winter solstice
A cloud of smoke is floating over the empire again
And sand and dust storms are sweeping across motherland
Ah, Poet, poet
Go on your pilgrimage to the palm of the green world

October 11, 2007. Princeton
(English Trans. Lucas Klein)

罌栗花
——加州感懷之一

綻開
飛翔的姿式——

如夢的水流
在柔軟的觸摸中
湧現，吟動

一隻螢火蟲點燈

天空奏響
盛大的音樂
斑斕，亮麗，暈眩——
群鳥扇形般竄起

葉片紛紛舞蹈
心臟鼓滿赤潮
茂盛的沃土
根莖蔓延

白色的天使
在幽暗的邊疆
呵門—
海濤翻卷
船舟逆流而上

Poppy Flower
——California Recollections NO. 1

Bursting forth
into a gesture of flight

Like dream of flowing water
With a soft touch
It rises up and chants

A firefly lights a lamp

The sky plays
grand music
colorful, bright, dizzy
A flock of birds flees in fan formation

Leaves dance around
The heart fills with the red tide
Luxuriant, fertile soil
Roots spread out

A white angel
At a dim frontier
knocks at the door—
Ocean waves spinning around
Boats go against the current

告別土地
告別腐爛的季節
告別有限實在
告別循環輪迴

空靈縱隊
飛翔──
風景啊
請展示你詩意的無限山水吧!

2002.6加州大衛斯

Farewell to this land

Farewell to this decaying season

Farewell to the limits of the Real

Farewell to karmic samsara

Ethereal column

Soaring Up—

Ah, landscape—

Reveals yourself as an endless poetic scene!

June 2002. UC Davis

(English Trans. Matt Turner and Haiying Weng)

詩人

詩人
策馬
千里迢迢
與大道竟跑
呼吸
迎風撲面的顫慄

那是繆斯的呼召

詩人
耕作
千山萬水
散播奇幻的糧食
打磨
天堂口的隕石

那是大地萌動的脊樑

詩人
練箭
日復一日
弓上鏗亮的弦
反射

The Poet

The poet
spurs the horse
a thousand miles on
races with the Dao
breathing
a thrill of shivering against the wind

This is the Muse's calling

The poet
tills
endless mountains and streams
sows fantastical grains
shines
the meteor at the gate of paradise

This is the backbone of the earth's germination

The poet
practices archery
day in and day out
The shiny string on the bow
reflects

持守者無畏的雙眼—

一輪天堂裡的明月

　　　　　　　　　　　　2006/2010於普林斯頓

the fearless eyes of the holder

A bright moon in paradise

2006/2010. Princeton
(English Trans. Matt Turner and Haiying Weng)

讀柳宗元《江雪》

千山鳥飛絕
萬徑人蹤滅
孤舟蓑笠翁
獨釣寒江雪

在一個酷熱的夏日
我讀完這一首古詩
心裡頓覺涼爽至極
當空的驕陽也化作飛雪

可是我很想知道
老柳何時寫下這首詩
是在炎熱的酷夏還是
在冰雪覆蓋的寒冬？

我也很想知道
老翁在小船上垂釣時
是否曾料到一位姓柳的詩人
將他寫進一首詩裡並名垂千古？

2010.12.20於普林斯頓

Reading Liu Zongyuan's River Snow

"Birds gone from the mountains
All trace of man gone from the paths
A fisherman in straw clothes in a lone boat
Fishing alone in the cold snow"

On a broiling summer day
After I finished reading this ancient poem
immediately I felt myself cooling down
and the blazing sun above also turned into snow

But I'd really like to know
When did Old Liu write this poem?
Was it in a scorching summer or
Was it in a freezing winter?

I also really want to know
When the old man was fishing on the little boat
Did he expect a poet named Liu
to write him into a poem and be passed on and on?

December 20, 2010. Princeton
(English Trans. Matt Tuner and Haiying Weng)

量詞操練
——四行大白話

1

一群沙丁魚遊過
又一群沙丁魚遊過
一條大鯊魚緊隨其後
別怕！這是我正在看的一幅畫

2

一群野鹿躍牆而過
又一群野鹿越牆而過
牆角一聲獵槍響起
一隻幼鹿倒牆而過

3

一群老鴨子大搖大擺過馬路
一群小鴨子簸顛簸顛過馬路
一排排汽車都停了下來
突然誰按響了一聲車喇叭？

Measure Words Drill
——Quatrains in the Vernacular

1

A school of sardines swims past
Another school of sardines swims past
A big shark follows hot on their heels
Don't be scared! This is a painting I'm viewing

2

A gang of wild deer jumps over the wall
Another gang of wild deer leaps over the wall
A rifle sounds from the corner of the wall
A fawn falls over the wall

3

A plump of old ducks swaggers across the highway
A plump of ducklings knock each other crossing too
Rows of cars come to a stop
Who honked their horn so suddenly?

4

一排野鵝在天上飛
另一排野鵝在水裡遊
忽然「咕咚」一聲
一排白脖子全栽進了水裡

5

四隻燕子前年從屋頂上飛過
三隻燕子去年從屋頂上飛過
兩隻燕子今年冬天從屋頂上飛過
可是今年春天一隻燕子也沒飛來

6

一隻松鼠爬上鳥籠吃玉米
又一隻爬上去一起吃
一隻紅雀鶇也飛來一起吃
「嘩啦」一聲，鳥籠掉了下來

7

一隻松鼠抓起一個小紅番茄，吃下
又抓起一個小紅番茄，吃下
抓到一個青番茄，吃不下
扔掉，跳上樹枝，嘴一抹就走了

4

A column of wild geese flies in the sky
Another column of wild geese swims in the water
Suddenly a thump
A column of white necks plunges into the water

5

Four swallows flew over the roof the year before last
Three swallows flew over the roof last year
Two swallows flew over the roof this winter
But this spring a swallow has yet to come

6

A squirrel crawls on a birdcage and eats corn
Another one crawls up and they eat together
A cardinal flies up and they eat together
With a clang the birdcage falls down

7

A squirrel nabs a plum tomato, and eats it
and nabs another plum tomato, and eats it
nabs a green one, doesn't eat it
casts it aside, jumps on a branch, wipes its mouth, and leaves

8

一片樹葉掉了下來
又一片樹葉掉了下來
大風一吹
樹葉全散了

9

一群黑螞蟻在路上爬行
一排紅蜻蜓在空中飛旋
一陣炸雷驚響
紅蜻蜓飛走了，黑螞蟻也不見了

10

兩隻老松鼠在樹幹上上竄下跳
四隻小松鼠在洞口東張西望
一陣颶風刮來
空地上裸出了一個大樹墩

11

1995年在青城山頂我吃了一頓美味的豆腐
那是老和尚親手做的
在山腳下我又吃了一頓美味的豆腐
這是農家小姑自己做的

8

A leaf falls down from a tree
Another leaf falls down from a tree
A great wind blows
The leaves all scatter around

9

An army of black ants marches on the road
A column of red dragonflies flies in the air
A burst of thunder explodes, startling
The red dragonflies fly away, and the black ants also disappear

10

Two old squirrels run up and down a tree trunk
Four little squirrels peer around the hole of a cave
A cyclonic gust blows past
A great stump is exposed in an empty lot

11

In 1995, at the peak of Mt Qingcheng, I ate some delicious doufu
It was made by an old monk himself
At the foot of the mountain I ate some more delicious doufu
It was made by a girl from the village

12

小時候我在一棵大槐樹上
刻下一個「米」字
多年以後槐樹不見了
可「米」字卻長了出來

13

夏天夜空滿天星星
嘉陵江裡也是漫江星星
突然一道彗星劃過
江裡星星一下就少了一顆

14

一隻蝴蝶飛來
無夢
兩隻蝴蝶飛來
無情

2010.12.15於普林斯頓

12

When I was young I engraved a 「米」
On a scholar tree
Years later the scholar tree was gone
But the 「米」 character had sprouted

13

Summer's night sky is full of stars
The Jialing River's also full of spilling stars
Suddenly a comet's tail streaks across
one star is missing from the river

14

A butterfly flies up
No dream
Two butterflies fly up
No passion

December 15, 2010. Princeton
(English Trans. Matt Turner and Haiying Weng)

2010年第一場雪

昨晚下了一場大雪
清晨打開屋門
一陣刺骨的寒風襲面
四周寂靜
松柏枝壓滿雪片
尖細的針葉俯伏地面

遠望草地
白棉花舒展
雪風吹拂
突然從飛白的花絮下
揚起一串串細細的
松鼠覓食的飢餓爪印
歪歪斜斜地
在樹墩後消隱

2010.12.27於普林斯頓

First Snow of 2010

There was a heavy snow last night
I opened the door in early morning
A peel of brisk wind slashed my face
Silence all around
Pine branches weighed down by snowflakes
Sharp needles lying all over the ground

I gazed over the lawn
White cotton was unfolding
Caressed by snowy wind
Suddenly, darting from the white catkins
A track of thin, slight
paw prints of the hungry squirrels, foraging
zigzagging
Disappearing behind the tree stump

December 27, 2010. Princeton
(English Trans. Matt Turner and Haiying Weng)

白卵石

一浪複一浪
滑行於激情的腹部
經千年柔媚的撫摸
誕生於蒼茫的藻行間

閃光如念珠
一串念誦的腹語
不可洞穿的天機
忽被鹹的巨鯨曝露

洶湧的突圍擊潰
萬年的堅固意志
時間之書分解，渴望
隨層層泡沫蕩上堤岸

如銀針的穿刺
團團白色的渾圓
在潮帶上劇烈翻卷
飛馬跨越棗紅的珊瑚

某些夏日的偶遇
這粒粒沁涼的潤滑
潛入我不安的排行中
成為今夜溫暖的凝視

White Pebbles

A wave follows a wave
sliding over a passionate belly
Through thousands of years of caresses
born among endless rows of algae

Flickers like a rosary
A string of words recited by a ventriloquist
The mystery that can't be pierced
suddenly exposed by a huge brackish whale

A violent surge breaks through
firm will of eternity
The Book of Time breaks down, longs
to follow layers of spume on the embankment

Like the puncture of a silver needle
Rounds of white shapely rounds
Whirling violently through tidal waves
A flying horse gallops over red coral

Some summer day's encountering
This grainy cool ooze
seeps into my restless enjambment
turns into tonight's warm gaze

然而，我是否已將她拯救
收留即與時間之水剝離
成為陸地的囚徒
被烈日無情地暴虐

好了，就這樣宣告吧：

與其讓酸雨腐化，還不如
將她拋回無底的汪洋，痛快地
任狂潮滌蕩，一層層，一圈圈
輪轉，磨損，直至渾身碎裂

　　　　　　　　　　　　2010.2.8於新澤西海洋林

But whether or not I have rescued her
To take in means to strip the water of time
To become a prisoner of land
and tortured ruthlessly by the burning sun

Alright, so I proclaim:

Rather than rot in acid rain, might as well
throw her back into the vast ocean, outright
washed away by the torrential tides, layers and circles
cycling, wearing down, until head to toe is shattered

August 8, 2010. Ocean Grove NJ
(English Trans. Matt Turner and Haiying Weng)

菩提花開

佛說：打開手掌，世界坦坦蕩蕩，開闊無邊，
握緊拳頭，裡面空空如也，盡是煩惱根和痛苦的輪迴；

大家都是熟透了的明白人，為什麼不敢面對這些卑微的跌絆呢？
大慈大悲為懷，何以如此絕情，連給人重生的機會都沒有？！

誰不委屈？誰不冤怨？人該清清白白，不可不白不冤，
原本早就參破這紅塵之無聊，何來這麼多煩惱！

放下吧，跨將過去，親愛的朋友，讓日子平常如初，
星空之下，人類何其渺小，如浮萍，無依無助；

昨夜秋風乍起，秋雨綿綿，霜冷長河，秋水寒心，
這是落葉蕭蕭的時節，親愛的朋友，這是渴求友情的時節；

這是一個真摯的懇求，鞠一個體諒的躬，親愛的朋友，
讓生活重新開始，縱然生命苦短，而菩提樹下終有暖暖的光芒。

2010.1.9於普林斯頓

Bodhi Blooms

Buddha says: Open your palm up, the world is wide-open and infinite ,
Clench your fist, all empty inside, and full of worry and samsaric suffering;

We are all sensible people, so why don't you face these petty stumbles?
One should have compassion in the heart, why do you behave so heartlessly?

Who hasn't felt wronged? Who hasn't been angry? People should be
clean and not be unjust,
For long ago I had seen through the morass of the world, so why came
so much trouble!

Let it go, step over it, my friends, and let the days live on as in the past,
Under the stars humanity is so small, floating like duckweed, rootless and
helpless;

Last night the autumn wind picked up, the rain was continuous,
frosty river chilled the heart,
Here comes the season of falling leaves, dear friends, a season to long
for friendship;

Here is my sincere plea, here is my bow for your consideration, my dear friends,
Let life recommence, though life is short , under the Bodhi tree there
is always radiant warmth.

January 1, 2010. Princeton
(English Trans. Matt Turner and Haiying Weng)

颶風！颶風！

（2012年10月29-30日兩天的「颶風桑迪／上帝」肆虐美國
東海岸，造成了巨大的災難。下面的四行微型組詩完全是
詩人本人的親身經歷，毫無深度詩化，純粹直白紀錄）

1

颶風　暴災
斷電　漆黑
十指入暗夜
空空，一無所獲

2

颶風暴吹
橫捲地上殘渣
樹上鳥窩癲狂
傳下揪心的嘰喳聲

3

海浪滔天
拍擊灣中的渡船
桅杆上旗幟嘩啦一片
魚游過水下寂靜的錨

Hurricane!Hurricane!

（On October 29-30, 2012, Hurricane Sandy ravaged the east coast of the US, wreaking disasters. The following four-line poems reflect my personal experiences of this natural disaster, without being deeply poetic, but a purely straightforward record）.

1

Hurricane, wreck
Power outage, pitch dark
Ten fingers into the dark night
All empty, nothing to hold onto

2

Hurricane blew hard
Sweeping away junk on the ground
Bird's nest rocked frantically in a tree
Down came heart-wrenching chirpings

3

The waves dash to the sky
Batter a ferry in the bay
Banner on the mast clattering in the air
Fish swimming past silent anchors underwater

4

黑雲壓頂

高速路上車輛狂奔

在天地交接的電閃處

一隻高大的野鹿竄出

5

紐約死寂

海水倒灌城區

空蕩的華爾街道上

肥胖的鼠群倉皇逃離

6

曼哈頓黑

百老匯暗

時代廣場空

自由火炬滅

2012.11.7於普林斯頓

4

Black clouds were pressing down
Cars were running wildly on the highway
at lightening flash that joins heaven and earth
A great wild deer leapt off

5

Deathly stillness in New York
Seawater flew backwards into the city
On empty Wall Street
Hordes of fat mice fled in a panic

6

Manhattan dark
Broadway dim
Times Square empty
Torch of Freedom extinguished

November 1, 2012. Princeton
(English Trans. Matt Turner and Haiying Weng)

一隻站在阿卡迪亞礁石上的海鷗

1

就這樣我們遠遠地對視著
連空氣也變得異常脆弱
我不敢向前挪動一步
生怕驚動你專心覓食
而你突然昂起尖犁般的喙
啄向空中，劃了一圈
接著發出幾聲「穀啊穀啊」
彷彿在說（其實我已領會）：
「外鄉人，來這幹嘛？」

2

那瞳孔的光芒，隨
浪濤翻滾，激動的翼
攪亂鏡頭的焦距，如
濺迸的水銀，撕碎
外鄉人的好奇心，令他
行走雲端，在霧中潛行
一片羽光忽閃忽現：
「吁，多麼徒勞的捕捉
外鄉人那出竅的靈魂」

A Seagull Standing on Acadia Shore Reef

1

In this way, we stare at each other from afar

Even the air becomes exceptionally fragile

I dare not advance a step

for fear of startling your foraging

Yet you suddenly raise your sharp beak

peck in the air, making a circle

and then sending out continuous "kittee-wa-aaake"

As if to say (in fact, what I understood to be):

"You outsiders, what did you come here for?"

2

The radiance of the pupil, it follows

the pulsing waves, the excited wings

disturb the camera's focus, it's like

a splash of mercury, rending

the outsiders' curiosity, makes him

walk in the clouds, slink in the mist

A piece of feather gleaming through obscurity:

"Oh, how pointless to catch

the out-of-body souls of the outsiders"

3

「嗨，您好，海鷗兄弟
很高興見到你，今天
我運氣真好，天氣也不錯
你也裝扮得很時髦
潔白的羽毛，還閃著光澤

來做個自我介紹吧：
我來自新澤西，當然更遠
來自中國重慶（那裡沒有海洋，
只有江河；那裡有滿街的火鍋
最近那邊也熱鬧轟轟）
我來留學，讀個什麼文學博士
（其實又辛苦又無啥用處）
然後就留了下來，在一所大學蹉跎

前些年拿了張綠卡（至今還是
中國公民，呵呵，挺愛國的）
而今人到中年，卻時常想回老家
聽說這裡山水很美，便來逛逛

就聊到這裡吧，現在輪到你了
（要不要咱們先握個手再說？不能說
中文不大要緊，鳥語也行）
你說呢？」……………

3

"Hi, hello,   brother seagull
I'm glad to meet you. Today
I'm very lucky, the weather's nice
and you're dressed very fashionably
with spotless plumage and their sheen

Let's introduce ourselves:
I'm from New Jersey, well, originally
Chongqing, in China (where there's no sea
Just a river; where there are streets full of hot pot
Where, recently, it's roaring with excitement)
I came here to study, got a doctorate in literature
(although it was toilsome and useless)
and afterwards I stayed, idling in a university

I got a green card a few years ago (though I remain
a Chinese citizen , hey, I'm patriotic, haha!)
and now I'm middle age, and often think of my hometown
I heard the landscape was beautiful here, so I came to look around
Alright, that's it, now it's your turn
(Should we just shake hands for now? If you don't
speak Chinese, it's not a big deal, bird language is ok)
What do you say?"·················

4

這墩臨海的巨大礁石
光禿，孤僻，清冷
跪拜洶湧的海洋
腹部任潮水沖洗

而你的降臨令這裡多麼不同
攫緊的腳爪令擁抱刻骨銘心
柔毛的撫摸令無情激昂狂飲
笨重的軀體也化作飛翔的輕

而在你展翅起飛的一剎那
我忽然瞥見在巨石頭顱上
你拉下的純白的糞粒
在陽光下爍爍閃光

2012.11.21-22於阿卡迪亞-普林斯頓

4

This giant boulder by the sea
Bare, solitary, detached
kneels to the tempestuous sea
Let the belly be rinsed with the tides

But your arrival has made this place so different
Your seizing claws etch the embrace into the heart
The caress of your down has made the heartless revelled
This clumsy body is dissolved into the lightness of flight

At the moment that you flap your wings and take off
I suddenly glimpse on the head of the boulder
the pure white dung you drop
glistening in the sun

November 21-22, 2010. Acadia-Princeton
(English Trans. Matt Turner and Haiying Weng)

夜行紐約

午夜，一個中國人行色匆匆
在濕漉的時代廣場上穿行
霓虹燈閃爍如亂竄的怪獸
攪亂街頭急促的呼吸
豔女郎的紅唇噴血如溶漿
吞噬著行人飢餓的胃
地面上冒出鴉片的氣味
刺激人群疲憊的神經

午夜，一個中國人在紐約穿行
他掠過燒板栗的黑人老哥們
開計程車的巴基斯坦小夥子
兜售假名牌的福建同胞們
戴雪白披肩的俄羅斯貴婦們
脫衣舞門前猥褻的皮條客們

午夜，一個中國人在紐約穿行
他周遭的世界嘈雜晦暗
可他行色匆匆，又匆匆
腦子裡在想寫一首中文詩
來表達他的孤獨與傷感
他一直在想紐約深夜十二點
正好是老家重慶的親人們
在打麻將吃火鍋曬太陽

Nightwalk in New York

At midnight, a Chinese man is in a rush
Passing through a dripping wet Times Square
Neon lights flicker like scattering beasts
disturbing rushed breath on the street corner
The red lips of a gaudy woman spew blood like lava
devouring the starving bellies of pedestrians
Smell of weed emanating from the ground
stimulating the fatigued nerves of the crowd

At midnight, a Chinese man traverses New York
He sweeps past the old black guys selling chestnuts
The Pakistani fellows driving a cab
His Fujianese compatriots selling fake designer goods
The Russian ladies wearing a snow-white shawl
The crude pimps in front of a strip club door

At midnight, a Chinese man traverses New York
The dim world around him full of noise
But he is in a rush, so he rushes
He is thinking about writing a Chinese poem
to convey his heartsickness and loneliness
He's been thinking, at midnight in New York
It's just about time his family in Chongqing is
playing mahjong and eating hotpot in the sun

初春，午夜十二點，
一個外鄉人在紐約穿行
這裡的周遭都與他無關，因為
他心裡在想著重慶正午十二點
嘉陵江面上
蕩漾的
春日
暖暖的
陽光

2011．4．11於紐約

Early spring, 12 o'clock, midnight

A foreigner traverses New York

His surroundings are irrelevant to him, because

his heart is in Chongqing at 12 noon

on the Jialing River

ripples of a

spring day

the warmth of

sunlight

April 11, 2011. New York
(English Trans. Matt Turner and Haiying Weng)

鑿道三行

道可道，非常道
道生一，一生二，
二生三，三生萬物

——老子《道德經》

序幕

常道不可以言說
常道也不可書寫
常道可以開嗎？

一

晨曦微白
串串晶瑩的朝露
滴在山徑旁的斧柄上

二

一匹棗紅馬嘶鳴
凜冽的寒氣
隨馬刺的撲騰濺起

三

山泉淙淙
山石的苔蘚上
浮出霍霍的磨刀聲

Chiseled Dao Tercets

The Dao that can be spoken is not the constant Dao

The Dao begets one, one begets two

Two begets three, three begets innumerable things

——Laozi, *Daodejing*

Prelude

The constant Dao cannot be spoken of

The constant Dao can also not be written down

Can the constant Dao be opened up?

1

Dim white dawn light

Strings of crystal dewdrops

drop on the axe handle on the mountain path

2

A chestnut horse neighs

Biting cold air

flares up with the galloping spurs

3

The mountain stream gurgling

over the moss on the mountain stones

arises the sharpening sound of a knife

四

斧柄在手
旋轉於空氣中
一陣馬蹄鐵踏響

五

斧柄嘩嘩
花徑彈開
馬刺踏出杜鵑的血

六

磊石從邊徑聚攏
斧柄劃出尺碼
馬蹄鐵響徹空道

七

白蝴蝶從酣夢中
醒來，頓然發現
翅膀上長出一道彩虹

八

八月的麥子
撤離天空
群鳥從草垛上嘩啦而過

4

Axe handle in hand

spins in midair

A puff of horseshoes treading

5

Axe handle swishing

Blossoming path was cut open

Spurs stomp out cuckoo's blood

6

A pile of rocks round up at the edge

The axe handle draws the size out

Horseshoes resound down the empty path

7

A white butterfly immersed in a dream

wakes up, and suddenly finds

a rainbow has sprouted from its wings

8

Wheat in August

evacuated from the sky

A flock of birds clatters past haystacks

九

空曠的田野
四面裸露
小田鼠蜷臥於犁溝

十

霜氣彌漫
行人躡步
犁耙酣睡於草垛

十一

水上結薄冰
打水漂的男孩
揮動他凍傷的右手

十二

大海茫茫無邊
一條小船支起白帆
迎著風，起舞前行

十三

大船疾駛而過
隨後翻捲的犁溝
淹沒了掌舵的把手

9

An open field

Exposed from all directions

A vole curled up in a furrow

10

Frost pervading

A traveler quietly passes

Hoe and trowel sound asleep in the haystack

11

Thin ice on the water

A boy skipping stones on it

Brandishing his frostbitten right hand

12

The ocean is vast and without end

A small boat flies a white sail

against the wind, dancing ahead

13

A ship surges past

making a furrow in its wake

drowning the tiller

十四

彗星劃出軌道
喧鬧的銀河黯然
黑洞張開靈敏的雙耳

十五

磊石，磊石
滾滾，磨出墨汁
山水生出煙的花朵

十六

火車夜奔於曠野
如突竄的螢火蟲
忽然在隧道口熄滅

十七

一隻白鶴飛落在樹頂
她的雙眼仰望藍空
春日的喜悅油然而起

十八

春雷昨夜炸響
人間酣睡一片
唯有紅松鼠打開了巢門

14

A comet cuts a path

The noisy Milky Way dims

A black hole opens two acute ears

15

Rockpile, rockpile

Rolling, grinding out ink

Landscape begets flowers of smoke

16

A train runs through the wilderness at night

Like a blinking firefly

suddenly extinguished at a tunnel's entrance

17

A white crane lands on a treetop

Her eyes look up at the blue sky

The joy of Spring spontaneously arises

18

Last night Spring thunder cracked

The world slept soundly

Only the red squirrels opened their nest doors

十九

春雨昨夜淅瀝而下
光禿的丁香花枝
在清晨露出丫丫的青綠

二十

從水中撈起的沙粒
又從指縫中漏下
水中現出一雙惆悵的眼睛

二十一

火山石，赭紅的瞳孔
被窺視的最深處
是那更火熱的熔液

二十二

天藍，藍天
無風，無雲，無聲
大地上無我亦無人

二十三

行走，行走，行行走走
走也行，行也走
清澈之水無倒影

19

Last night the Spring rain tapped down
Bare lilac branches
Green buds were exposed in early morning

20

Grains of sand scooped from the water
leaking through the fingers again
A pair of melancholy eyes appears in the water

21

Volcanic rocks, ochre pupils
The deepest place that has been spied upon
is the more fiery lava

22

The sky is blue, a blue sky
There's no wind, no clouds, no noises
So are no people no self on the earth

23

Walk, go, walkwalk gogo
Walking is going, going walking
There's no reflection in the clear water

二十四

白孔雀，春日的白孔雀
後花園裡彩屏飛揚
頓覺落櫻滿南山

二十五

弦音滑向皚雪
黑釉如飛狐
奔瀉於蒼茫的雲際

二十六

雪覆蓋的莊稼地
移動在上面的是
扇形的野鵝掌印

二十七

太陽被陽光遮蔽
大海被海浪淹沒
天空被暴雨覆蓋

二十八

暴風雪鋪天蓋地
困頓在家的花貓
腳掌猛抓透亮的玻璃

24

White peacock, white peacock at spring day
Colors fly up in the back garden
Suddenly cherry blossoms are falling at South Mountain

25

The sound of the string slides across glimmering snow
Black glaze like a flying fox
rushing on the endless clouds

26

Snow blanketing the field
Moving over top are the prints of
wild geese in fan formation

27

The sun is shaded by sunlight
The ocean is drowned in waves
The sky is covered by a rainstorm

28

A blizzard covers sky and land
At home is a trapped cat
Paws pouncing on translucent glass

二十九

要觸摸水的清涼度
你得尾隨游魚的眼睛
持續下沉，下沉

三十

把耳朵罩住，把雜音濾除
深深地呼吸，讓肺葉擴張
耳花盛開，傾聽內心的梵音

2015.4.22-2017.12.31於耶魯-普林斯頓

29

If you want to feel the coolness of water
You need to follow the eyes of the fish
continue going down, going down

30

Cover the ears, filter the noise
Breathe deeply, let the lungs expand
The ears will bloom, listen for the chanting of the heart

April 22, 2015. Yale/December 31, 2017. Princeton
(English Trans. Matt Turner and Haiying Weng)

詩人除草機壞了

詩人北鳥想除草，
可除草機壞了；
我想出力幫他，
最後也莫辦法；

詩人現在不再窮了，
他有一棟漂亮的房子，
還有一座挺大的花園，
可詩的除草機卻壞了。

春意盎然，鳥語花香，
詩人醉心於革命與酒瓶；
詩箋黴灰生揚，詩草雜橫
因為詩人的除草機壞了。

2015.4.20於普林斯頓

The Poet's Weeder Is Broken

Poet Bei Niao wants to weed,
But his weeder is broken;
I'd like to help him out,
though it ends in vain;

The poet isn't poor any more,
He has a beautiful house,
and also has a big garden,
But the poem's weeder is broken.

Spring's in the air, birds tweet and the air's sweet,
The poet's obsessed with the revolution in a wine bottle;
The bookmark grows moldy, and poems and weeds mingle
Because the poet's weeder was broken.

April 20, 2015. Princeton
(English Trans. Matt Turner and Haiying Weng)

抄《本草綱目》

1.合歡

合歡，落葉喬木，豆科，高可達16米，
樹皮呈灰褐色，平滑，枝條粗而短；
葉互生，偶數二回羽狀複葉，夜間成對象合，
6-7月開花，頭狀花序，淡紅色，
合歡多長於向陽坡或灌木叢中。

合歡樹皮乾燥，名合歡皮，性平，味甘，
可消腫止痛，活血，續經骨，也可治失眠，
氣鬱胸悶，跌打損傷，肺痛。

合歡的總花梗頭狀花序，名合歡花，
性平，味苦，可養心安神，開胃理氣，
合歡的種子，名夜合子，乾燥，可治失眠，
《神農木草經》將合歡列入中品。

點評：大凡靈丹妙藥須經合歡，採陰陽之氣，
　　　滋肝潤肺，葆春催情，乃宇宙之天機也。

2010.10於普林斯頓

Copying the Compendium of Medical Herbs

No. 1 Silk tree

Silk tree, a deciduous tree, leguminous, grows to 16 meters tall,

The bark is gray-brown, flat and smooth, its braches rough and short;

Leaves alternate, are in even numbers, and close in pairs at night,

It blooms in June-July, in small cluster which is red,

The Silk tree often grows on a sunny slope or bush.

Its bark is dry and called Silk tree bark; a mild temperament, and sweet taste,

It can relieve swelling, aid blood circulation, strengthen bones, as
    well as treat insomnia,

regulate *qi* in the chest, heal fractures and lung pain.

The head of the Silk tree flower is conical, and it is called Silk tree flower

It has a mild temperament, tastes bitter, and can ease the mind and stimulate *qi*;

Silk tree seeds, called Night Closers, are dry, and can cure insomnia,

The Classic of Herbal Medicine categorizes Silk tree as middle-grade.

Commentary: Any effective miracle cure will use Silk tree to gather qi
    from yin and yang,

nourish the liver and moisten the lungs, and stimulate the sex drive.

This is the secret of the universe.

October, 2010. Princeton
(English Trans. Matt Turner and Haiying Weng)

2012年冬天第一場暴雪紀事

雪是晚上下的，有十六英尺厚，
早上打開房門，門口已經封凍，
先用靴子掀開小口，再找雪鏟，
撬開一條道，石板路寒風咧咧。

先瞥見一隻小松鼠吊在樹杆鳥籠上，
猛吃玉米粒兒，一定是餓極了，
松鼠瞧見了我，急忙跳下樹枝，
跑到另一棵大樹下繼續吃，
爪上捧著食物，兩隻眼睛直盯著我。

女兒拿出剛買的雪滑板，說「滑雪去！」
她興奮地把身體俯在雪板上，
來回滑動，嘴裡不斷念叨，「太棒了！」
雪板在積雪的街道上很快滑走，
女兒說，「鏟雪車來了就不好玩了。」

女兒建議我們去旁邊的公園玩雪，
她在雪地上寫下「Coco IS Here!」
說「等我們回來時，這些寫字就被雪蓋上了。」
半個小時後，我們返回時，那些字真不見了。

Chronicle of the First Winter Blizzard of 2012

It snowed at night, sixteen feet thick,
Open the door in the morning, the doorway's frozen solid,
First use boots to open a small hole, then find a snow shovel
Pry open a passage, a cold wind whines over the flagstones.

The first thing I see is a squirrel hanging on a birdcage on a tree,
Cramming kernels of corn, it must be starving,
The squirrel sees me, jumps down from the branch in haste,
runs over to another tree and continues eating,
Food in its claws, staring right at me.

Daughter takes out her new snowboard, and says "Let's go sledding!"
Excited, her whole body leans over the sled,
Sliding back and forth, she keeps exclaiming, "Terrific!"
Sled slides away down the snowy streets,
And daughter says, "When the snowblower comes it won't be any fun."

Daughter suggests we go to the park nearby to play in the snow,
She writes on the snow, "Coco IS Here!"
Says, "When we come back, these letters will be covered in snow."
Half an hour later we come back, and the letters have disappeared.

女兒又跟鄰居的好朋友去學校斜坡上滑雪，
一群小孩子帶上各種滑板，在坡上上下滑行，
堆雪障礙，互相比賽，摔倒又爬起，
雪花紛紛，人影模糊，但聞人語聲。

天色漸晚，女兒與同伴玩累了，
大夥兒踩著深雪，低一腳，矮一腳，
拖著雪板回家，不時還碰見熟人，
打一聲招呼，「哇，雪真大呀!好好玩兒吧！」

到了家門口，門又被雪封上了，
鏟開積雪，還好，只是雪花，易鏟，
進屋，關上門，眼鏡朦朧，擦拭，
聽見汽車紮雪吱吱駛過空街道，
據天氣預報說，今晚仍降大雪。

小女兒驚奇地問道，「那明天做什麼？」
我一邊脫靴子，一邊擦眼鏡，
然後對著鏡子哈了一口熱氣，
看著凍紅了雙頰的女兒，回答說，
「明天我們又滑雪去，怎麼樣？」

2012.12.26於普林斯頓

Daughter goes with her good friend to sled on the slope at the school,

A group of kids carrying sleds slide up and down the slope,

Making snow obstacles, competing with each other, slipping and
falling and climbing up again,

Snowflakes one after the other, blurred figures, only hearing the
sound of human voices.

The sky dims, daughter and her companion tire of playing,

Everyone stepping in the snow, one foot goes in deep, one in shallow,

Dragging the sleds home, still running into people we know,

Calls out a greeting, "Can you believe the snow's so heavy? Have fun!"

Arriving at the front door, which is covered in snow again,

Shovel it, it's a bit better, it's only snow, so it's easy,

Enter the house, shut the door, eyeglasses are hazy, wipe them,

I hear a car squeak over the snow in the empty street,

According to the weather forecast, there's more snow tonight.

My daughter asks in wonder, "What will we do tomorrow?"

I take off my boots while rubbing my glasses,

and then blow hot air onto the glasses,

Looking at the two cold red cheeks of my daughter, I reply,

"How about we'll go to sled again tomorrow?"

December 26, 2012. Princeton
(English Trans. Matt Turner and Haiying Weng)

政治波普詩

1.抄《毛主席語錄》

> （1970年小學一年級的教室裡，
> 傳出陣陣抄毛語錄的沙沙聲，
> 一遍又一遍，一頁又一頁，
> 一天又一天，一年又一年）

好好學習，天天向上；好好學習，天天向上；好好學習，天天向上；
好學好習，天向天上；好學好習，天向天上；好學好習，天向天上；
好好習學，天天上向；好好習學，天天上向；好好習學，天天上向；
好習好學，天上天向；好習好學，天上天向；好習好學，天上天向；
好學好習，天向上天；好學好習，天向上天；好學好習，天向上天；
（繼續抄‥‥‥‥‥‥‥‥‥‥‥‥‥‥‥‥‥‥‥‥‥‥‥‥‥‥‥‥‥）

哪裡有壓迫，哪裡就有反抗！哪裡有壓迫，哪裡就有反抗！哪裡有
壓迫，哪裡就有抗反！哪裡有迫壓，哪裡就有抗反！哪裡有迫壓，
哪裡就有抗反！哪裡壓有迫，哪裡就反有抗！哪裡壓有迫，哪裡抗
就有反！哪有裡壓迫，哪反裡就有抗！哪壓裡有迫，哪反裡就有
抗！哪壓裡有迫，哪就裡有反抗！哪有壓裡迫，裡就有哪反抗！哪
有裡壓迫，哪就有裡反抗！
（繼續抄‥‥‥‥‥‥‥‥‥‥‥‥‥‥‥‥‥‥‥‥‥‥‥‥‥‥‥‥‥）

Political Pop Poems

1.Copying from The Quotations of Chairman Mao

(In first grade class in 1970,

Rustling from copying the quotations of Mao emerges,

Again and again, page after page,

Day after day, year after year)

Study hard, progress every day; study hard, progress every day; study hard, progress every day; stud hardy, pro every daygress; stud hardy, pro every daygress; stard hudy, eprovery daygress; stard hudy, eprovery daygress; stard hudy, eprovery daygress; stud hardy, pro day every gress; stud hardy, pro day every gress; stud hardy, pro day every gress; (copyingcontinues···)

Where there is oppression, there is resistance! Where there is oppression, there is resistance! Where there is oppression, there is anti-resistance! Where there is anti-oppression, there is anti-resistance! Where there is anti-oppression, there is anti-resistance! Where pressure is applied, there is anti-anti! Where pressure is applied, where resistance is anti-! If there is oppression, there is resistance to it! If there is pressure on the pressure, there is resistance to it! If there is pressure on the pressure, where there is resistance! Where there is pressure, there is resistance in it! If there is oppression, where there is resistance!
(copying continues···)

下定決心、不怕犧牲、排除萬難、去爭取勝利。下決定心、不犧怕牲、排萬除難、去取爭勝利。決下定心、怕不犧牲、排萬除難、去勝爭取利。下決定心、不犧怕牲、難排除萬、爭去取勝利。決下定心、不犧怕牲、萬排除難、去爭勝取利。下心定決、犧不怕牲、排萬除難、去勝爭取利。下決定心、不犧怕牲、排萬除難、去取勝爭利。決下定心、犧不怕牲、排萬除難、去勝爭取利。下決定心、牲不怕犧、排萬除難、去爭勝取利。

（繼續抄‥‥‥‥‥‥‥‥‥‥‥‥‥‥‥‥‥‥‥‥‥‥‥‥‥‥）

敵人一天天爛下去，我們一天天好起來。敵天人一天爛下去，我天們一天好起來。爛敵人一天天下去，起我們一天天好來。敵下人一天天爛去，我們一起天天好來。天敵人一天爛下去，我好們一天天起來。敵爛人一天天下去，我們一天來天好起。敵下人一天天爛去，我起們一天天好來。敵人一去天天爛下，天我們一天好起來。敵一天人天爛下去，我一天們天好起來。敵人一爛天天下去，我們好一天天起來。

（繼續抄‥‥‥‥‥‥‥‥‥‥‥‥‥‥‥‥‥‥‥‥‥‥‥‥‥‥）

2.聽寫

某老師，同學們，聽寫開始了，請認真聽：

（世界是你們的，也是我們的，但是歸根結柢是你們的。你們青年人朝氣蓬勃，正在興旺時期，好像早晨八九點鐘的太陽。希望寄託在你們身上。）

Be decisive, fear no sacrifice, overcome all difficulties, strive for victory. Be indecisive, sacrifice no fear, it is difficult to overcome difficulties, get to strive for victory. Settle down, fear not sacrificing, it is difficult to overcome difficulties, strive for profit. Be indecisive, sacrifice no fear, it's difficult to rule things out, fight for victory. Settle down, sacrifice no fear, eliminate difficulties, strive for victory and take profit. Sink to the bottom, do fear not livestock, eliminations are difficult, strive for victory and take profit. Be indecisive, sacrifice no fear, eliminations are difficult, win and fight for profit. Settle down, do not fear livestock, eliminations are difficult, strive for profit. Be indecisive, livestock do not fear sacrifice, eliminations are difficult, strive for victory and take a profit.

(copying continues······)

Each day the enemy gets worse and then we get better. If the enemy gets worse then we continue to get up. If the enemy goes down then every day we'll rise. The enemy goes down every day so we get up together. The enemy goes down so one day we'll get better. When the enemy goes down we get up and its good. The enemy gets worse and we all get better. The enemy gets worse daily and one day we'll all get up. The enemy of the people gets worse so one day I'll get better. When the enemy goes down we better get up.

(copying continues······)

2. Dictation

A teacher says, Students, dictation has begun, please listen carefully 」 :

(The world is yours, it is also ours, but, eventually, it will be yours. You young people are full of vigor, full of potential, like the sun at eight or nine in the morning. Hope depends on you.)

死界是你們的，也是我們的，但是歸根結底是你們的。你們青年人
朝氣蓬勃，正在興旺時期，好像早晨八九點鐘的胎陽。虛妄寄託在
你們身上。

3.給毛主席點煙

偉大領袖毛主席嗜煙如命
他老人家一生抽過：
葉子煙，旱煙，紙煙，捲煙
「555」牌洋煙，「熊貓」
「中南海」以及特製的132雪茄
毛主席說：「吃百家飯，抽百家煙」

毛主席煙癮超強，無人能及
據說他一天抽50根煙
然而，不抽煙也能發威
1945年在重慶與老蔣談判時
因蔣介石不抽煙，更厭惡煙味
毛主席在期間便抑制了抽煙
據說這一強力意志震懾了蔣總座

兒時別人崇拜戴紅五星八角帽的毛主席
而我特別崇拜抽著煙的毛主席
不是嘴裡刁著煙的毛主席
而是用食指與中指夾著煙的那位
我深深感到兩指間夾著的蘇修美帝
便在偉大領袖的抽吸中煙消灰滅

The dead world is yours, it is also ours, but, eventually, it will be yours. You young people are full of fucks, full of potential, like fetuses at eight or nine in the morning. Delusion depends on you.

3. Light a Cigarette for Chairman Mao

The Great Leader Chairman Mao loves smoking as his life
This old man has smoked all his life:
Leaves, tobacco, cigarettes, cigars
"555"foreign brand, "Panda"
"Zhongnanhai" as well as the specially made "132" cigar
Chairman Mao said: "Beg for food, beg for cigarettes"

Chairman Mao was a chain smoker, second to none
It's said that he smoked fifty cigarettes a day
Even not smoking, however, can be also intimidating
Like when he negotiated with Chiang Kai-Shek in Chongqing in 1945
Because Chiang didn't smoke, and he detested the smell
Chairman Mao restrained himself from smoking during that time
It's said that his strong will awed Generalissimo Chiang

In childhood, others adored Mao with the red-starred octagonal cap
But I especially admired Chairman Mao in smoking
Not Chairman Mao with a cigarette in his mouth
But the one with a cigarette between the fore- and middle fingers
I felt that Soviet revisionism and American imperialism between his two fingers
were extinguished to ashes in the Great Leader's inhaling and exhaling

每當看到煙火在主席指間忽明忽暗熄滅
我就夢想著我能為主席點下一根煙
某夜恍惚我終於見到了毛主席
「毛主席，您好，我能為你點一隻煙嗎？」
「當然囉，小夥子！」
只見主席彈出一支煙，夾在兩指間
「請點吧，小夥子」
「主席，我不敢點」
「呵呵，為什麼？怕什麼囉？」
「我不敢燒中南海」
「哈哈，中南海只是一個牌子，一張紙而已」
聽主席一席話，倍感鼓舞
我便斗膽擦亮了火柴，為主席點了煙
看著「中南海」在主席指間燃燒至煙蒂
「你看看，小夥子，中南海不就是一張紙嗎！」
我很高興我今天為毛主席做了一件好事

許多年以後，1976年9月9日
偉大領袖毛主席去世了
據說因抽煙過多死於肺炎
這個噩耗如晴天霹靂，令我悲痛欲絕
我後悔我不該為毛主席點煙
致使他老人家得了絕症
我好自責，深感我害了他老人家
然而，雨過天晴，彩虹當空
我頓覺我為中國人做了一件大好事

2017.13.15-31於普林斯頓

Every time I saw smoke flickering between the Chairman's fingers

I dreamed that I could light a cigarette for the Chairman

One night, in a trance, I finally met Chairman Mao

"Hello, Chairman Mao! Can I light a cigarette for you?"

"Of course you can, little boy!"

The Chairman popped up a cigarette and held it between his two fingers

"Go ahead, little boy"

"Chairman, I don't dare"

"Oh? Why? What are you afraid of?"

"I don't dare set fire to Zhongnanhai"

"Haha, Zhongnanhai is a brand, just a piece of paper"

On hearing the Chairman's words, I was heartened

I ventured to light a match, and lit the cigarette for the Chairman

I watched "Zhongnanhai"burnt down to embers between the Chairman's fingers

"Look, little lad, isn't Zhongnanhai only a piece of paper?"

I was very glad that I did a good job for Chairman Mao that day

Many years later, on September 9, 1976

The Great Leader Chairman Mao departed the world

He allegedly died of pneumonia caused by his excessive smoking

and the sad news was like a thunder clap, squeezing at my heart

I regret that I lit a cigarette for Chairman Mao

and contributed to this grand old man's terminal disease

I felt so remorseful for having harmed this man

Nevertheless, after the storm comes the blue sky and, look! A rainbow

I suddenly felt that I did a great thing for the Chinese people

January 15-31, 2017. Princeton
(English Trans. Matt Turner and Haiying Weng)

曼哈頓懸日

如
一個
紅透的
柿
子
旋動
火
球
呼哧呼哧
鮮
裸
肉汁
濺
迸
灑遍酒精
滾
翻
烈火熊熊
燒
爆
汽油
彩虹的金勺
喧譁
晚宴
吐出大舌頭

Manhattanhenge

Like

a

red hot

per-

simmon

a swirling

fire

ball

puffing panting

fresh

bare

nectar

squirting

gushing

spraying alcohol

roiling

flipping

blazing fire

burning

exploding

gasoline

a golden spoon rainbow

a tumult

a banquet

sticks the big tongue out

將

銀河的雲煙

一

吸

而

盡

克萊斯勒腹部的油膩光澤
映照格網大道翹首的奇觀者
隨薩克斯低顫的迷幻布魯斯
目擊帝國沉陷的灰燼
傾聽大洋滔滔的弦音

2011.7.10於紐約

inhale

the clouds of the Milky Way

all

in

one

breath

The greasy luster of Chrysler's belly

Illuminating the grid's curious spectators

A hallucinatory blues trembles with the sax

Witness the embers of a sinking empire

Listen to the ocean's surging crescendo

July 10, 2011. New York
(English Trans. Matt Turner and Haiying Weng)

望氣歌樂山

1985-1995

Cloud Divination on Mount Gele

盲女

門譁然關閉
乳泉中倒立著我胎中的背影
洶湧的泡沫隨黎明的紅桔生長
群鳥從水上喚來一枝枝黑色的蘭草
路，一條光亮的飄帶，從我手上滑過

黑暗降臨，我在月光的影子裡終日蝸居
我撲在地上，以手當爪
在與時間的周旋中，我的面孔
成了木梯上高懸的果實
　　那永久的碩果，噴泉上紅紅的雲片
　　在正午，與夢中光亮的森林相遇同焚

期望的火焰閃現，火鳥
滿天起舞，「時機到了！」
我不聞不問，觀著濕潤的月
從天窗中洩出，水，一片光燦
晝夜啄蝕古堡緊閉的門
　　鼓聲錚錚，春祭的天鵝環樹而行
　　雨夜，黑蝴蝶傾巢湧出孤寂的谷罅

「太久遠了，」如仙女的渴望
我清瘦的面龐從水簾中消隱
和風起伏的溪流中，蓮花迎水而來
那個時節，秋雨也紛紛入池

Blind Maiden

The door clangs shut
Water dripping from stalactites mirrors the upside-down shadow in my fetus
Raging foam grows with the red-orange dawn
On the water, a flock of birds summons stems of black orchid
The road, a shimmering ribbon that slips through my hands

Darkness falls, I nestle in moonlit shadows all day long
I throw myself on the ground, using my hands as claws
In the whirl of time, my face
becomes high-hanging fruit on a wooden ladder
  That eternal fruit, reddish clouds on a fountain
  At noon, meeting and burning with the bright woods in a dream

The flame of an expectant longing flashes, a firebird
dances in the sky, 「It's time!」
I remain indifferent, staring at the wet moon
spilling through the skylight, water, a beam of light
day and night pecking at the closed gate of an old castle
  Drums clatter, as in a rite of spring, swans circle round the tree
  A rainy night, black butterflies swarm out of the lonely valley

「It's too far away,」 like the yearning of a celestial maiden
My emaciated face vanishes in the cascade of water
In a stream rippled by the warm wind, lotus flowers greet the current,
  floating to and fro

棲宿在洞穴中披彩的女人，回首遠望
無波的水上又響起了漲潮的笙歌
　　十月的岸邊，燕子揀芳草居石而巢
　　　船夫殺鹿塗血棄舟
　　　在子夜掀起的鵑聲中
　　　告別了枯水的路
　　………………………………

　　　　　　　　　　　　1987.3於重慶歌樂山

In this season, autumn rain pours into the pond in heavy drops
The colorfully dressed woman who lives in a cave turns back, gazing
　　into the distance
The still water resurges with the music of the swelling tide
On the bank in October, swallows gather fragrant grasses and make
　　nests out of stones
　　The boatman kills deer and smears blood on the abandoned boat
　　At midnight, the cry of the cuckoo rises
　　Says goodbye to the dried-up road
　　..

March 1987. Chongqing Mount Gele
(English Trans. Jennifer Feeley)

鳥在黃昏

鳥歸回之際
黃昏漫過燈塔幽暗的邊緣
如夢的渴望回答著我
我摸索著
試圖找回一種不復存在的印跡
或者歸入印跡的啟示中去

子夜的暈月使我回想起
正午突然悸動的鐘擺
馬車從遠方駛來，車輪
切開河岸與冰的距離，游魚
閃示出我出生時食指的預言

一種奇特的弧形文字
旋轉於天空
促發潮汐洶湧，殘陽飲水
而當我沿岸溯上
仰觀終級時
飛鳥沉寂，退讓並祈求消失

悄悄潛伏在季節的暗流中
宛如石頭
祕密的深度更替時間
重複慧星體內痛苦的音樂
午夜的鴿子被囚禁

Bird at Dusk

At the time when the bird returns
dusk brims over the dim edge of the lighthouse
Dream-like yearning answers me
I fumble around
Trying to find an irrecoverable trace
or merging into the revelation of this trace

The halo around the moon at midnight reminds me of
the pendulum that suddenly throbs at noon
A carriage comes from afar, wheels
slicing open the distance between the riverbank and ice, swirling fish
flickering with the prophecy of the index finger when I was born

A strange, arc-shaped word
whirls in the sky
arouses the surging tides, the setting sun sips water
While I follow the shore and go upstream
glancing up at the ultimate end
Soaring birds keep quiet, retreating and praying to vanish into air

Silently lurking in the undercurrents of the season
Like a stone
Secret depths replace time
Repeat the painful melody of comets
Midnight pigeons are imprisoned

車輪旋轉
黃昏的鐘擺回答著我的名字

1986.11於重慶歌樂山

Wheels keep turning

Dusk's pendulum answers my name

November 1986. Chongqing Mount Gele
(English Trans. Jennifer Feeley)

世紀末：風・雅・頌

雅風之一

河流向下——
水上漂著樹葉；
根向下——
鮮花勃發在空中；
果實向上——
發在風的芳香中流；
雅風，雅風，
我心愛的小妹妹——
在水中洗著閃光的黃金。

風雅之二

船在河中——
女人在船裡——
夢在葉脈上
一種野味在生長。

四月，芽在地下，
女人如初醒的游魚，釋放
一股醉人的氣味——
請飛翔吧！我春天的情人。

Fin de Siècle: **Popular Ballads • Festival Odes • Sacrificial Songs**

Elegant Air 1

The river flows down—

Leaves drifting on the water;

Roots point down—

Flowers bloom in the air;

Fruits point up—

Hair blows in the fragrant wind;

Elegant airs, elegant airs,

My darling younger sister—

Rinsing glittering gold in the water.

An Air of Elegance 2

Boat in the river—

Woman in the boat—

Dreams on the veins of leaves

A kind of wild game is growing.

In April, buds underground,

Like an early awakened spawning fish, a woman emits

An intoxicating scent—

Please fly! My spring lover.

風／雅之三

酒在樹上──
糧食在地下──
火在溫度中──
節日裡蕩漾著華彩的女人

在根莖下面舞蹈，掀開
土壤，在白色的斷裂處──
溢出泉水，瓊漿與火苗──
以及騎著駿馬，奔向天堂的女人。

雅／風之四

雅風之聲，
漫過洶湧的麥浪──
在天際，
有南瓜在滾動──

渾圓的銅鑼，
拍打著鄉村的柿子──
在秋天，我聽見
雅風，在國土的珍珠雨中紛紛傳頌。

Air/Elegance 3

Booze on the tree—
Grains underground—
Fire in the temperature—
A colorful woman rippling in the festival

Dancing beneath the rhizome, splitting open
The soil, in the white rupture—
Bubbling springs, nectar and flames—
and the woman who rides the steed, galloping to heaven.

Elegant/Air 4

The sound of elegant airs,
spilling over the billowing waves of wheat—
At the horizon,
a pumpkin rolls—

A perfectly round brass gong,
beating the village persimmon—
In autumn, I hear
an elegant air, singing out in the pearl rain of the country

風／雅之五

時間在流放——
書卷只翻開第一頁——
昨夜，地上一片白霜，
哦，朋友上征途，
步履之聲響徹遠方。

沒有燈塔，沒有舟子，
那不是我們的家鄉：
孤獨的流水，焰火與洞穴——
哦，時間飢餓，
根正飲沼澤之水。

雅／風之六

橘子切開一半，
滾向另一邊地球；
牙齒在桔黃的葉輪中，
剪碎青春的彩條——

乳燕在銀河上穿梭，
點燃盞盞華燈——
讓天空兩邊，
飄滿夢幻的羽毛。

1994.10.12於香港中大

Air/Elegance 5

Time in exile—
The book only turned to page one—
Last night, there was a coating of frost on the ground,
Oh, friends setting off on a journey,
The sounds of footsteps echoing in the distance.

There's no lighthouse, there's no boat,
That's not our homeland:
Lonely drifting water, fireworks and caves—
Oh, time is starving,
The roots are drinking swamp water.

Elegant/Air 6

The orange is cut in half,
rolls to the other end of the earth;
Teeth are caught in the orange impeller,
cutting up the colorful ribbon of youth—

The young swallows shuttle across the Milky Way,
lighting lamp after lamp—
filling both ends of the sky
with floating dreamlike feathers.

October 12, 1994. CUHK Hong Kong
(English Trans. Jennifer Feeley)

偶然之鳥

風雨中的樹
在粉紅色的水波裡
紛紛暴動；

披髮的少女，
撥動神經與骨頭，
用火的身體，
在七月的鏡波中，
接受洶湧的沐浴；

神聖的黑髮翻卷，
清洗不美的塵土，
提升日常的鹽，
在水的潮流中，
一隻飛動的大鳥
翱翔在你如夢的星空。

裸之歌聲，
撒向四方八面，
穿越在我的十指間──
一種顫慄，一陣升騰：
幸福萬萬年！

1994.5.7於香港中大

Accidental Bird

Trees in the rain
In the pink ripples
riot one by one;

The messy-haired woman,
fiddling with nerves and bones,
uses a fiery body
in the mirror of waves in July
to welcome a raging bath;

Sacred black hair flutters,
cleans the unpretty dust,
raises the daily salt
In the swirling water,
a large bird flies
soaring in your dream-like starlit sky.

A naked song
spreads in all directions
passes through my ten fingers—
A shudder, a sudden surge:
thousands of years of happiness!

May 7, 1994. CUHK Hong Kong
(English Trans. Jennifer Feeley)

節日的鏡子

太陽開花了
那黃金的麥穗是否
仍懸在你的鏡中
眼睛，在另一面鏡子裡
越過花叢，穿越白色的水銀

消息隨綠葉而至
我的季節也是你的季節
說話或沉默
群鳥在空中交流

當白色成為我們的深處
當語言成為我們的風暴
說話或沉默
回憶或未來
我美麗的凝視已成為
你高傲的眼神

太陽開花的時候
節日在水銀中
鏡子在火焰中
眼睛在群鳥中——
你是花朵還是黃金？

1992.10於香港中大

Holiday Mirror

The sun blooms
Are those golden ears of wheat
still hanging in your mirror
Eyes, in another mirror
pass through flowering shrubs, pass through white quicksilver

News arrives with the green leaves
My season is also your season
To talk or keep quiet
A flock of birds communicates midair

When white becomes our depths
When language becomes our storms
To talk or keep quiet
Memories or the future
My beautiful gaze has become
your proud eyes

When the sun blooms
Holiday in quicksilver
Mirror in flames
Eyes in a flock of birds—
Are you a flower or a piece of gold?

October 1992. CUHK Hong Kong
(English Trans. Jennifer Feeley)

秋歌之一

哦！想起來了，我的愛人
想起我怎麼分開你的樣子
而為這一永久的姿勢，我要為此
一生痛苦，在心中絞痛

好讓果核孕育，這核中之核
便是一個中心，倆人合圍，
一個果核的心臟，越變堅硬
如海螺中的波濤
我們在其中接受沐浴

一百年的功夫，就鑄煉成了
光明？光明中的核心
黃金的心臟，時間永遠敗退
啊，想起來了，我要為這
孕育之母痛苦一生

在果實中孕育，在黃金中痛苦
因為我的缺席，我不敢仰視
樹巔之果，而在我低頭之際
一種聲音，一種果核進裂的聲音——
啊！愛人，這是地獄也是家園

Autumn Song No. 1

Oh! I remember, my beloved
Remember the way I separated you
into this eternal pose. For this
I'll suffer a lifetime, aching in my heart

So as to breed the kernel, the heart of the heart
is a center, two people circling around,
The heart of the kernel grows harder
Like waves in a conch
we bathe in it

A hundred years of effort tempered into
light? The kernel of brightness
heart of gold, time forever retreating
Ah, I remember, for this
mother of life I'll suffer a lifetime

Breeding in a fruit, suffering in gold
Because of my absence, I don't dare glance up at
the fruit at the top of the tree, and while I bow my head
a sound rings out, the sound of a kernel splitting open—
Oh! My beloved, this is hell as well as home

秋氣蔓延，我夢想中碩大的光明
橫掃藍空，在果實輝煌的透亮中
我想起了，想起了
我出來的地址還能回去麼？
哦！果實！黃金！我的孕育之母。

                                          1990.10於北大

Autumn air unfurls, the great brightness of my dreams

sweeps the blue sky, in the brilliant transparency of fruit

I remember, I remember

Can I still go back to that old dwelling?

Oh! Fruit! Gold! My mother of life.

October 1990. Beijing University
(English Trans. Jennifer Feeley)

秋歌之二

又起風了——
樹葉落了下來，
顏色落了下來，
——紛紛落進我的書中

關上書本，我冥想著未來
竟發現一字不識——
一個純粹的盲人

一氣之下，我扔掉了書本
用水果刀劃碎了字典
狠狠地關閉了圖書館大門
我來到了大果林下——
「聽——風！」

起風了，好大的季節風在林間灌響
猶如「嘩嘩」旌旗，
我的全身被震盪著
全部內心的表現被掏空
「知覺？」在白色的洶湧裡
「空白？」空白無邊無際——
一片透明的木葉
一道燦爛的光彩
一隻進裂的果子
落

Autumn Song No. 2

The wind blows again—
Leaves fall,
Color falls,
—Falls into my book one after another

I close the book, wonder about the future
Surprised not to know any word—
A pure blind person

In a fit of anger, I throw out the book
smash the dictionary with a fruit knife
slam the library door
I end up underneath a large fruit orchard—
"Listen to—the wind!"

The wind blows, the great seasonal gust roars through the grove
Like the rustling of a flag,
My whole body shakes
My insides are all hollowed out
"Perception?" In the white surge
"Blank?" Blank and boundless—
A transparent leaf
A brilliant glow
A shattered fruit
Come

了
下
來
——紛紛落進我身體之內

終於，
親切的，精確的，直接的

在我再現的還原中
我看清了那個神祕的詞——
事物！僅僅事物而已！
其餘皆成問題。

1990.12於北大

Fall-

-ing

Down

—Falling into my body one after the other

At last,

Intimate, precise, direct

In my retrieving recuperation

I make sense of that mysterious word—

Things! Merely things!

Everything else becomes extra.

December 1990. Beijing University

(English Trans. Jennifer Feeley)

秋歌之三

在秋天，
道路綿延，灑滿閃亮的雨，
如風的歌聲從頭上飄過，
從一片片的雲朵中——
我聽到了你如歌的流水。

在秋天，
你來自清亮的雨水，
如一只動情的小金魚——
透澈，歡欣而神祕，
遊嬉，奔動在我黑暗的發中。

芬芳啊，芬芳！我美麗的欲望，
在雨水中清洗，翻騰，
在我雙目發光，穿透祕密時，
你是一個歡快的小精靈，飛翔—
在秋天。

這又是一個令人珍愛的時辰——
在秋天，我夢見了你，
在果實奔放而升騰的頌歌中，
是你，清亮的小金魚從遠的途中，
給我帶來一生的夢：蘋果與黃金。

1994.10.26於香港中大

Autumn Song No. 3

In autumn,
The road stretches on, awash with glistening rain
A wind-like song wafts past my head,
From tufts of clouds—
I hear your song-like flowing water

In autumn,
You come from the clear rain,
Like an excited little goldfish—
Transparent, joyful and mysterious,
Playing, darting around my black hair.

Fragrance, oh fragrance! My beautiful desires,
washed in the rain, surging,
Shining in my eyes, when secrets are penetrated,
You are a cheerful little elf, soaring—
In autumn.

This is another endearing hour—
In autumn, I dream of you,
In the song of the fruit vibrating and rising
It's you, clear little goldfish who's come from afar,
Bringing me a lifetime of dreams: apples and gold.

October 26, 1994. CUHK Hong Kong
(English Trans. Jennifer Feeley)

秋歌之四

切開一只水果，
冬天就要來了。

盤子裡無需耕作，
這裡瓜熟蒂落，
收穫重歸泥土，
這裡沒有秤砣。

候鳥越過天際線，
天空不再做夢，
打開果園的柵欄，
人們搬進了巢穴。

1994.10.28於香港中大

Autumn Song No. 4

Cut open a fruit,
Winter is coming.

There's no need for farming on the plate,
Here a ripe melon falls from the stem,
The harvest returns to the soil,
Here there is no scale.

Migratory birds cross the skyline,
The sky no longer dreams,
Cut open the orchard fence,
People are moving into the nest.

October 28, 1994. CUHK Hong Kong
(English Trans. Jennifer Feeley)

晌午之樹

晌午之樹淹沒花園

陽光正鋪張寬宏
在一日復一日的頷首中
洗淨不真實的思想
把異地的行為
奉還健康和精神

　　畫像歸為身體
　　晌午之樹突起理想
　　構思一日復一日，虛幻的詞
　　飾滿簇葉之巔，卜示
　　古道的真跡和險景

信任啟示英雄的靈感
讓生日的淚水祈求心聲
祈求靠進人們關懷的臉
晌午陽光溫和
簇葉飽漲情思
撫愛無間親密
隨著一日復一日的自由
美好終將溢出真誠的白雲

A Tree at Noonday

At noon, a tree drowns the garden

The sun spreads out its magnanimity
In the nod of day after day
washing away untrue thoughts
giving back the behavior of a strange place
to health and spirit

The portrait returns to its body
At noon, a tree suddenly emits ambition
Conception breeds day after day, illusory words
crowned with tufted leaves, divining
authentic and dangerous scenes of the old path

Trust triggers heroic inspiration
May birthday tears pray for the heart
Pray to be closer to people's caring faces
The noon sun is mild
The leaves are in the mood for love
Fondling the infinite intimacy
With the freedom of day after day
Beauty will flow from the sincere white clouds

晌午，花園中湮滅了一棵樹
一棵輝煌的樹，讓人們永遠銘記

　　　　　　　　　　　1987.7於重慶歌樂山

At noon, a tree is destroyed in the garden

A brilliant tree, may people forever remember

July 1987. Chongqing Mount Gele
(English Trans. Jennifer Feeley)

月光謠

（一）

經歷，風雨中難眠
勾起長思，讓歲月的光
穿過手掌厚重的編織，多少次
飛鳥的哀呼，肢解了
多少個星雲般的夜晚
聲音和河流聚合，在圖像中
記憶燃起白色的火焰，把
泛灰的古舟推向依稀的遠方

（二）

誰迎接了你
風，為了別的季候
經過夏日的牆沿
拂去路上所有的標向

帽簷的紅縷搖動
誰恐然發現
牆沿邊一隻手
從注視的水波上
伸向藍色的柵欄

我來自另一個世界

Moonlight Ballad

1.

Experiences! How hard for me to sleep during a storm
It stirs up lingering memories, makes the light of the years
pass through my thickly woven palm prints, so many times
The mournful cries of flying birds, dismembered
so many nebulous nights
Sounds and the flow of the river converge, in the image
Memory ignites a white flame, pushing
the old graying boat into the hazy distance

2.

Who greets you
Wind, for other seasons
passes along the wall of summer days
whisks away all of the signs on the road

The hat's red tassels are shaking
Who is frightened to find
a hand on the edge of the wall
From atop the waves of the gaze
stretching out toward a blue fence

I come from another world

（三）

　　　初春之夜
你挪進柴垛，傾心於如故的暗香
　　　踏步依然，聲音亦如斯
你百感交集，讓衣袖溫暖
　　　霜中的枝頭

風靜悄，夜亦深
你呼吸逝去的時辰，卻看見
一隻貓猛然竄過，零花落滿斑紋

（初春之夜
月光散亂於塵土上
你踏去在遠方的征途
異處的芬芳是否依然如故，亦如斯？）

沐浴之水從心上淌過
我呼吸到了一股溫暖的芳香
從你純白如練的袖中蕩來

1983-1985-1987於重慶歌樂山

3.

Early spring day
You stumble into a stack of firewood, fall in love with its scent déjà vu
Stepping in place like you used to, the same is true of the voice
You have mixed emotions, let your sleeves warm up
Boughs in the frost

The wind is silent, the night is deep
You breathe the time that has passed, but see
a cat suddenly darts past, its strips strewn with fallen petals

（An early spring night
Moonlight scatters on the dust
You embark on a long journey
Is the scent of different places still the same?）

Baptizing water courses through the heart
I catch a whiff of a warm fragrance
swaying from your white silk sleeves

1983-1985-1987. Chongqing Mount Gele
(English Trans. Jennifer Feeley)

緬懷秋天

前些日子，有故人重訪，因而談起了秋天
想起了黃昏時的梧桐葉和蘆葦中緊張的風
像期待了許久，也整日爭吵不休
掩卷的面龐一直沉默不言，貓來了
在雪地裡潛伏伏爪的氣味，暗示越來越深
聲音無端地擴展，出走既艱難又危險
唉，秋日親切的女兒，我深深地思念
明日我能重返秋天？

　　　　（跛步的老人消失，
　　　　　　道路正憂鬱……霧）

想起了往年，秋意很濃
我紮上了背包帶，說是去遠征
那陣子秋雨很好，清涼的水正涉過金色白樺林
而為了長大，我也正害著超越白樺的夢
至今年華長得多麼高，而仍恪守升騰的誓言
外面鳥兒高飛，天空難以企及
聽見秋水的話語，那個秋天已遙遠

　　　　（道路模糊，
　　　　　　日子漂移……冰）

故人辭別西去，下午我空閒，心情優柔
望著窗外匆匆行人，一前一後，一來一往

Reminiscing about Autumn

A few days ago, an old friend dropped by again, and so we talked about autumn
Recalling the buttonwood leaves at dusk and the tense wind in the reeds
As if we'd been expecting it for a long time, yet arguing nonstop the whole day long
The folded face remained silent, the cat showed up
The scent of its claws lurking in the snow, omens growing deeper and deeper
Sound expanded for no reason, running away was difficult and dangerous
Alas, my dear daughter of autumn, how I deeply miss it
Tomorrow can I return to the autumn?

（The pacing old man vanishes,
　　The road is gloomy—fog）

Recalling years past, thoughts of the autumn are dense
I put on my backpack, claiming that I'm going on a trip
That fine spell of autumn rain, cool water fording the golden birch forest
In order to grow up, I too am obsessed with dreams of surpassing the birch trees
Thus far, the years have grown so tall, still keeping the oath of ascension
Outside, the birds soar high, the sky is hard to reach
Hearing the mutter of autumn water, that autumn has already sailed far away

（The road is hazy,
　　The days drift—ice）

My old friend said goodbye and went west, in the afternoon I was free, unhurried
Staring out the window at pedestrians rushing by, in tandem, back and forth

猛然想起故人離去的步態，秋天的步態
白樺林前撫琴的少女，羞容可掬
雖說遲到的時刻已逝去許多，然景色仍如初秋
看一看時間和橋下流水，小學生放學了，歡歌笑語
六點鐘，古銅色的馬車正滾向遲暮的深秋

　　　（木葉呆呆，一粒金黃的麥子
　　撒進雪裡，隨水，完成另一個更燦爛的合圍）

　　　　　　　　　　　　　　1986.10於重慶歌樂山

I suddenly recalled the gait of my old friend leaving, the gait of autumn

A young maiden strumming the lute in front of the white birch forest, bashful

Though the late hour had passed long ago, the scenery was still like early autumn

I looked at water flowing under the bridge, little kids out of school, singing and laughing

Six o'clock, the bronze carriage rolled toward the twilight of late autumn

(Wood leaves glittering, a grain of golden wheat sprinkled in the snow, with water, completing another even more brilliant circle)

October 1986. Chongqing Mount Gele
(English Trans. Jennifer Feeley)

海棠花

你駐紮，從河的另一岸
而彷彿在秋天
從容如風，潔淨如裙角
可能很委屈，也還悒鬱

風景隨流水
遙想昔日父親的厚愛
你怎不熱淚滿襟
一出生就高貴
和季節一起享受至上的特權

許多年風風雨雨
你也忠誠，而為了諾言
你整日以幻想安撫影子
從河的另一岸
前來尋捕那盞燈的消息

而有人說河岸正在退移
暗示並不在秋天

1985.9於重慶歌樂山

Begonia

You are stationed on the other side of the riverbank
As if it were autumn,
Calm like the wind, clean like the hem of a skirt
Perhaps you feel wronged, not to mention depressed

Scenes flow with water
Reminiscing about your father's love from bygone days
How can you not be full of tears
Noble by birth
Enjoying the highest privilege with the season

Year after year of wind and rain
You are loyal, you keep your promises
You spend your days placating shadows with fantasies
From the other side of the riverbank
Come to catch news of the lamp

Some say the riverbank occurs receding
Revelation is not in autumn

September 1985. Chongqing Mount Gele
(English Trans. Jennifer Feeley)

石弦

那只能是你

從虛空的夜，使
木葉發出火的濤音

悠長，從不需應和
完美的進吐如玉碎珠落
懸淵的呼喚使耳膜顫慄

誰發現了你，聽見了你的脈動
又清晰，又模糊
風帆和搖櫓，在黎明前
呈現給你太古的形象，滾動的

幽思已撫眠千年，鹿角
刺開大蟒林的路
通向更堅深的迷誤，太陽沒落
月光在你的黑髮中變為古謠曲，等待
與太陽一起躍出固定的永恆

Stone Flute

That can only be you

From the empty night, making
the leaves roar with flames like crashing waves

Drawn out, no need for any correspondence
The perfect spout like the tinkling of jade and pearls
The call of the abyss makes eardrums tremble

Who discovers you, hears your pulse
Clear, and yet vague
Sails and oars, before the dawn
present you with an ancient image, rolling

Thoughts have lain dormant for a thousand years, antlers
pierce the road in the python forest
leading to deeper loss, the sun has set
Moonlight becomes an old tune in your black hair, waits
with the sun to leap out of a fixed eternity

你永不會短促，你永遠靜止
你固守，從不消耗
消耗就是生長，生長有限的生命
你只能合併，去相會一聲
無限的終止，與自己的衝動
完成對空氣的包圍和顯示

顯示生命，顯示對美的領悟
你空亮的律動，掀開無祕密的軀體
使鳥兒的羽毛紛紛脫落，在空中
幻成透明的氣味，號召的光
燃亮了迷誤，那條通往廟宇凋破的路
鹿群棲止於岸邊，準備啜飲
一種宏大的聲音，從沉船的桅杆上升起

　　　　　　　　　　　1986.5於重慶歌樂山

You'll never be brief, you're forever still
You cling to yourself, never consume it all
Consuming it all is growth, growth has a limited life
You can only merge, go meet with
limitless termination, with your own impulses
resulting in the encircling and revelation of air

Showing signs of life, showing an insight of beauty
Your empty rhythm uncovers the body without secrets
makes birds shed their feathers, in the air
giving off a pure smell, evocative light
ignites the chaos, that abandoned road leading to the temple
Herds of deer perch on the shore, preparing to drink
a grand voice, rising from the mast of the shipwreck

May 1986. Chongqing Mount Gele
(English Trans. Jennifer Feeley)

受傷的玫瑰

鐘聲，
宛如一個懷孕的寡婦
憂鬱而至，
星空，
投下……一條長長的背影，
在秒針上啜泣。

澄澄水波憂傷地漫過月鏡之門，
美麗的房間，頓然
星光點點。

1982.10於重慶歌樂山

Wounded Rose

The peal of bells,
like a pregnant widow
arrives with melancholy,
starry sky,
casts off a long silhouette,
sobs on the clock's secondhand.

Crystal-clear waves sadly spill over the moon's gate,
beautiful room, suddenly
lit with stars.

October 1982. Chongqing Mount Gele
(English Trans. Jennifer Feeley)

春花時代
——現代敘事詩之一

山中，杏花節又款款來到
溫暖的雨掀開霧的道路
你佇立在暗紅的山門
讓舒展的髮結隨山風蕩漾
或者讓領須被松濤灌注
木魚的喧聲正鼓動群山
你鬆開心緒，行步羊齒草叢
你盼望山下平靜的穀禾和人家

你認真又愛人
本該享受一個溫暖的家園
（撫愛快樂的孩子，種植豐饒的糧食
過著普通人適意的生活），然而
你恨那個狠心的男人
為了虛幻的信仰，他捲入了不分勝負的混亂
在狂熱的昏眩中他喪失了幸福的責任

藍天傳遞季節循環而憂鬱的消息
你在青春的狩獵中把穀穗懸在鏡子裡
日夜思念廣遼的原野
撫摸秋天一天天變涼的印花毛巾
退卻的湧動留下一片恐懼與悲哀
你凝望崎嶇的山道
你不願延伸這紛亂的命運

The Age of Spring Flowers
——Modern Narrative Poem 1

In the mountains, the apricot festival comes again
Warm rain lifts the foggy road
You stand at the crimson mountain gate
Letting down your hair to ripple in the mountain breeze
Or letting your collar be suffused with the soughing of pines
The clamor of the wooden fish agitates the mountain range
You relax your mind, trample on ferns
You long for the peaceful crops and family beneath the mountain

You're earnest and loving
deserve to enjoy a warm home
(Caress happy children, plant a cornucopia of food
Live an ordinary, agreeable life), but
You despise that cruel man
For his false beliefs, he is drawn into a winless chaos
In his crazed dizziness he loses his right to happiness

The blue sky transmits the season's cyclical and sad message
In the hunt of youth, you hang ears of grain in the mirror
Day and night, you miss the vast open plains
stroke the patterned towels of autumn that grow colder by the day
The surge of retreat leaves behind a trail of dread and grief
You gaze at the rugged mountain pass
You don't want to extend this turbulent fate

在孤單的冥想中
你突然想起了山中如歌的鼓聲和偈語
你清醒憂慮，當黃昏投下嚮往的火苗
你踏上了深遠的青石階

五年一晃，十年也煙霧而過
你整日埋伏種籽，居住在杏樹林裡
以鮮花照耀天空，以果實撫愛心房
你在親切的自然中築造公正的良心
把學校的知識給予松，草和土地
於是你的愛情浮動土壤，靈感燃燒草叢
而松葉，松花和松果也因你的鍾愛
隨清晨的潮水湧向你快樂的身體

在更痛苦的種植裡
你決心重新生長，奉獻鮮嫩的果實
使知識滋生欲望，使自然袒露情意
做著變化的夢，哼著山歌
在黃昏燃燒的最後一個夜晚
你擁抱了另一個影子
一個將在杏花節如光彩的華蓋向你呈放
向你啟示一條通往石頭，森林以及果實的道路
你估量著，並開始了撤退

In solitary meditation
You suddenly recall song-like mountain drumbeats and Buddhist hymns
You're free from worries, when dusk casts off the flame of longing
You tread on far-reaching blue stone steps

Five years pass in a flash, ten years pass like smoke
All day you lie in wait planting seeds, living in the apricot grove
Blazing the sky with fresh flowers, caressing the heart with fruit
In kind nature you build a just conscience
Giving all you've learned in school to the pines, grass, and land
So your love upturns the soil, inspiration burns grass
and because of your care, pine needles, pine blooms, and pinecones
surge toward your blissful body with the morning tide

In the even more painful planting
You resolve to grow again, offer fresh fruit
Knowledge breeds desire, nature bares its affection
Dreaming of changing, humming mountain songs
The last night of dusk burning
You embrace another shadow
A glorious canopy is presented to you in the apricot festival
Leading you to a path toward stone, forest, and fruit
You size it up, and start to retreat

四月的和風雨淅瀝而下
山巒整夜奏著燦爛的春曲
鮮花開放在河流上，人們
湧向陽光，成群結隊
結著黑髮，裝束美麗
在正午松木林中來回閃爍
掌燈時分，無人扣門
女人撫琴頌歌昂揚

霜橋上，是那人踏來
花期臨近了

　　　　　　　　　　　　1987.9於重慶歌樂山

The pitter patter of April breeze and rain

The mountain range plays brilliant spring tunes all night

Flowers bloom on the river, people

flock to the sun in large numbers

Tie back their black hair, dress to the nines

Twinkling in the pine forest at midday

When the lamp is lit, no one raps at the door

A woman strums the lute, plays lively songs

That person steps on the frost-covered bridge

The season of blooms is near

September 1987. Chongqing Mount Gele
(English Trans. Jennifer Feeley)

秋日幻景

白雲深處，老荊夫
放下負擔
登上一座向南的峰頂
觀看落日
聆聽海水沉沒的潮音
讓願望在芬香的信仰中終身固定
暮夕寧靜，他喜悅的目光中
升起了遠村的燈火與果園
他激動，擁抱幸福的衣裳
隨晚風飽嘗完美的景色

一個安詳的中心正在形成
散失的老駿馬紛紛歸來
老荊夫極目遠望，雲海翻滾
他揮手迷茫之霧
卻看不見時間與流水
空寂的心如轉動的幻景
老荊夫在偉大的幻思中
變成了另一個人——
奔波歲月，觸摸所有的道路
把木輪扛在肩上
沿著漫長的石階，裸露回憶的卵石
在雞鳴的回聲中，尋覓回家的路

Autumn Mirage

Amid the white clouds, the old woodcutter

puts down his load

climbs to the top of a south-facing peak

watches the sunset

listens to sunken tidal sounds

May his wishes be eternalized in the fragrant faith

Twilight tranquil, in his joyful gaze

The lamps and orchards of a faraway village raise up

He is excited, embraces his blissful clothing

enjoys the perfect view in the evening breeze

A peaceful center is forming

Lost old steeds gallop back in droves

The old woodcutter stares into the distance, the sea of clouds rolls

He waves among the misty fog

But can't see time and flowing water

Empty heart like a whirling mirage

The old woodcutter in a grand fantasy

becomes someone else—

runs through the years, touches all the roads

shoulders a wooden wheel

Along the endless stone steps, pebbles of bare memory

search for the road home in the echo of the rooster's crow

終南山的秋天，雲高氣爽

一隻疲倦的獅子枕著松木

正做著大團圓的夢

山道上，老荆夫挑著黃金的植物

眼含淚水

又望見了遠處斫木的村落

1987.6於重慶歌樂山

Autumn in the Zhongnan mountains, high in the clouds with fresh air
A worn-out lion rests its head on a pine
dreaming of a big reunion
On the mountain path, the old woodcutter picks golden plants
His eyes brimming with tears
He stares at the distant villages where all the wood has been chopped

June 1987. Chongqing Mount Gele
(English Trans. Jennifer Feeley)

野菊花飄香

一句叮嚀的話遙遠

四月的手
輕靈地
搭起春天的帳篷
一片倨傲
土壤高漲溫情的目光
侍候
友人的衣領和筆

一杯酒埋在地下
搖來搖去

一九八七年一個男人
靜坐窗前
侍候一隻筆和一個女人
五月的下午，一個女人
思想興昂
捎來去年九月溫涼的酒

一句叮嚀的話遙遠而至

1987.5於重慶歌樂山

Scent of the Wild Chrysanthemum

An exhortation from afar

April's hand
deftly
sets up a spring tent
a piece of haughtiness
The gaze of soil surges with tenderness
attends to
friends' collars and pens

A glass of wine buried underground
swings to and fro

1987, a man
sits in front of a window
attends to a pen and a woman
One May afternoon, a woman
joyfully
delivers cool wine from last September

An exhortation arrives from afar

May 1987. Chongqing Mount Gele
(English Trans. Jennifer Feeley)

季節

不知探詢新消息的人走遠了沒有
聽說有一條峽谷
不會跨過藤樹搭成的獨木橋
讓我們等待吧
消息可能還很遙遠
街上的行人不會關注夜裡走廊的足音
即使有什麼快要消亡
黃昏依然歸去

日子在雞蛋裡努力
似乎並不企求什麼
縱使有一次山崩
也不會塗改河流的標向
風向標，預示著
我們得從一個房間穿越另一個房間
日子不會等待
窗子就要乘風飛去
日曆卷起了，彷彿
有人仍在等待

蘋果固然很美麗
樹葉總是懸著
要想回到彼岸
就得更換衣著，猶如
枯樹發芽

Seasons

I don't know whether the news-inquiring person has gone far away

I heard there is a gorge

that can't cross the single-log cane bridge

Let's wait

The news may still be far off

Pedestrians on the street won't notice the footsteps in the night corridor

Even if something is about to die

The dusk still returns

Time labors in the eggs

Don't seem to ask for anything

Even if there's a landslide

It won't change the course of the river

The weathervane indicates

We have to pass from room to room

Days will not wait

Windows sail away in the wind

The calendar rolls up, as if

someone is still waiting

Apples are undoubtedly beautiful

The leaves are always hanging

Wanting to go back to the other shore

You have to change your clothes, just like

Withered trees sprout

月亮失落
錢塘江漲潮
這一切都不可期待
季節尚未動身
人群來回往復
讓我們等待吧——
風向標的啟示
遠方帶來的消息

　　　　　　　　　　1984.4 於重慶歌樂山

Moonlight spills

The tides in Qiantang River rise

None of this is to be expected

The season has not left yet

The crowd moves to and fro

Let's wait—

The weathervane reveals

news from afar

April 1984. Chongqing Mount Gele
(English Trans. Jennifer Feeley)

造訪者

夜色如灰貓，此時我倚著那棵樹
盼著三個人的來臨
一個我在路上相遇過的
一個我已多年遺失的
一個我在夢中交談過的
對於我，他們像遙遠的晨星，既熟稔又陌生

那一個我在街上見過的，粉紅的顏色
屋簷下雨滴的絳色傘，正揣著微涼的步子
斜側的腰身，凝望濕髮上沉灰的天空，然後
用乳白的圍巾拂開胸前的團霧，躲閃的手
拒絕明亮的祝福，背棄古渡頭難忘的懷舊

懷舊，如水上的星撲溯，恰似多年以前
從水上飄去的木屐，而今又隨漲潮歸來
我多年遺失的那一個也要歸來嗎？帶著漂泊的孤單
和風夜的愁楚，復活那程端莊的流連
那雙我已多年遺忘在深巷裡苦惱的畏縮

像兩隻小灰鴿，爬上今夜小屋裡
鬆軟的小木梯，撫慰我悸動的雙手
安穩我菊花般的心緒，夜光如風鈴般飄逸
原來我夢中交談過的那一個，是我多年遺失的
在街上，我相遇過的，我那年冬雪中的顫慄

1986.6於重慶歌樂山

Visitors

Night is like a gray cat, now I'm leaning against the tree
Awaiting the arrival of three people
One I met on the road
One I lost many years ago
One I talked to in a dream
To me, they are like distant morning stars, familiar yet strange

That one whom I met on the road, colored pink
The crimson umbrella that drips under the overhang, with a slightly cold gait
Waist slanted, gazing at the dusty sky above wet hair, then
brushes away the fog with a creamy white scarf, hands dodging out of the way
refuses the joyful blessing, abandoning the unforgettable nostalgia at the old ferry

Nostalgia, a star fluttering against the current, just like many years ago
The wooden clogs floating on the water now wash up with the tide
Will the one I lost many years ago return? With drifting loneliness
The melancholy of the windy night evokes the demure lingering
That pair of troubled winces I'd forgotten many years ago in the deep lane

Like two small gray pigeons, climbing into tonight's small house
The soft wooden ladder soothes my throbbing hands
Smoothing my chrysanthemum-like mood, moonlight fluttering like windchimes
The one I talked to in a dream is the one I lost many years ago
On the road, we met, that winter the shiver I had in the snow

June 1986. Chongqing Mount Gele
(English Trans. Jennifer Feeley)

和歌
——給DL

來自漲潮的遠方，你
為了分擔，顫動起多年
眼中的憂倦，並真心更改
忘掉陣痛的雙腳和雨中的錯落

難得有豐盛的時間，平靜記憶
讓淚水洗淨委屈的塵埃
使卑怯化為書中執拗的花朵
如火的詢問，跳動著
碰觸某個祝福的生日
在鏡中印下懇求的心跡

嗚咽使語言猜度雨中的失意
多少回低頭的憂思，探首的悔悟
也拾不起謙遜中冰涼的蘋果臉
因和善的相聚，你創造過應變的機智
而信念的吊橋仍如輕揚的雨片
無聲地滑落

Correspondence
——For DL

From the rising tide afar, you
for sharing the load, flicker the worries and fatigues
in your eyes for years, and willingly go for a change
forget two painful feet and the untidiness in the rain

You barely have luxuriant time to calm memory
Let tears wash away the dirt of grievance
Transforming timidity into willful flowers in books
Inquiry is like fire, bounding
touching the earnest motive in a mirror
imprinted by a certain blessing birthday

Weeping makes language guess the frustration in the rain
You lower down for deep meditation, and look up for repentance
Not able to pick up your ice-cold apple face in humility
For the kind reunion, you've created the wits of flexibility
Whereas the suspension bridge of belief slips down silently
like those raindrops drifting lightly

應該記起雨燕中那棵樹
在寧靜的守約之後
穿過透明的雨簾
喚進舊日迷戀的和歌
和故園慈愛的路

「回家的路啊！」
河水湯湯，
隔岸有人呼喚你

　　　　　　　　　　1986.7於重慶歌樂山

You should remember that tree in the rain of drifting swallows
After the silent observation of promise
move through the transparent curtains of rain
call to sing the enchanting old songs
and walk on the road of love in your hometown

「 The road leading home! 」
The river is rushing by,
someone is calling on you from the other side.

July 1986. Chongqing Mount Gele
(English Trans. Feng Yi)

春天的庭園

一條曲折的小徑，切開
幽深的青竹林
桃葉片閃出背蔭處的惡言
如不可替換的老牆的鏽釘
昨天圍牆外退掉的泥土，而今
繡出了綠色的花朵，密謀遍佈時間

誰也不可想到，一場微雨，三點二點
會在牆院中心，埋下一棵樹籽
種植堅實的信念，使春天膽怯
那邊起伏的石階，正起步走向
遠方，一扇從未開啟的門
默默地恭候著古代征士的歸來

路避開密謀的刀劍，驚起
隱去的蟬聲，多日塵封的窗戶
突然飄出書的香味，被遺忘的歲月
引發內疚和歎息，逝去的多情季節
孕出了成熟的堅果，在初晴的節日裡
使鏽釘退落，使春天又芬芳

1985.9於重慶歌樂山

A Spring Garden

A zigzag path cuts through
a deep bamboo forest
Its leaves flicker over the hateful words in the shade
Like that irreplaceable rusty nail in the old wall
Yesterday, the earth retreated from the wall, yet today
Embroidered green flowers, a conspiracy permeating time

No one expects it, that a light rain, some drizzle
will bury a tree seed in the center of the yard
and plant a firm faith, make Spring timid
The undulating stone steps begin to go
and far away, a door that has never been opened
silently waits for the return of the ancient warriors

The road avoids the conspiring sword, shocking
hidden cicada chirping, a window layered with days of dust
suddenly the fragrance of books wafts up, the forgotten years
cause guilt and sighs, seasons of passion past
nurture the nuts to maturity, on the first sunny holiday
Let the rusty nails fall back, and let Spring be fragrant

September 1985. Chongqing Mount Gele
(English Trans. Matt Turner and Haiying Weng)

祈風

從遙遠的地方，橡樹林的風
經過長途的刻求，帶給你
萬頃真情的注視，倦飛的綠色鳥兒
流淚於橋頭，焦渴，並期待著
木筏上奏起水的笛聲，富饒而和諧

不是這樣嗎？從遙遠的地方
往事的那一年匆匆來到，在雨中
定下相會的日子，而風的鳥兒
卻偷走相會者的名字，你默守著，
日夜盼望雨中淅瀝的足音

光陰如流水
霧中的影子悄然飄過橋頭
而你正終日苦守，忠心於眼淚
你與風定下相會的日子
就定下了未來祭奠的那把火苗

忍耐的風從遠處吹來
在橋頭，尋找水的和聲

1986.10 於重慶歌樂山

Praying to the Wind

From a faraway land, the wind of oak trees
through the long distance, brings you
a thousand gazes, a tired green bird
shedding tears on the bridge, thirsty, and anticipating
the flute of the water playing on the raft, rich and harmonious

Is that not true? From a faraway land
That year from the past came hastily, in the rain
The day to meet was set, but the birds of the wind
stole the name of the returnee, so you waited silently,
Day and night hoping for the foot patter of the rain.

Time is like running water
The shadow in the mist slipping across the bridge
You've been waiting, loyal to the point of tears
The date you set to meet with the wind
also set the flame for the future memorial

The wind of patience blows from afar
on the bridgehead, looks for echoes of water

October 1986. Chongqing Mount Gele
(English Trans. Matt Turner and Haiying Weng)

軌跡

許多年，
小孩兒踏過了，
那條春花的道路，
留下了滿天紅色的雨點，
在依稀地眷戀著晴天。

許多年，
老人們穿過了，
那條烏鴉的河流，
灑落了萬點孩兒般的眼睛，
在焦慮地尋捕著日神，
啊，許多年。

許多年，
遊戲做完了，小孩兒
鬆弛了握緊的放牛繩，
邁步在草帽與陽光的邊沿，
病狂的夜空便頃刻
氾濫出老人們踱步的背影。

許多年，
即使你滿面憂傷，
其實我們都彼此理解，
你踮著踔步如薄霧，
我們頃刻間已誤解了許多年。

Pathway

For many years,
Children have stepped over
the road of spring flowers,
leaving the sky full of red raindrops,
longing hazily for sunny days.

For many years,
Old men have passed through
the river of the raven,
scattering thousands of childlike eyes,
and anxiously hunting for the sun god.
O, so many years.

For many years,
The game has been over, the child
loosens the tight grip on the reigns,
walks on the edge of the straw hat and the sunshine.
The sickly night sky instantaneously
overflows with the shadows of old people pacing.

For many years,
Even if you are sad –
In fact, we understand each other.
You stand on tiptoe like a mist, and
instantly we have misunderstood many years.

因過度厭倦，
許多年，誰也不首先抬頭，
觀看江岸的萬家燈火，
彼此都揣著許多不愉快的往事，
冥想著午後的鐘聲早已沖淡紅色雨點，
啊，還是許多年。

其實許多年，
路軌早已合圍了，
那條秋葉蕭蕭的甬道和雨中期切的眼神，
只是你忘記了秋風中微溫的面頰，
哭泣，卻又無望地期待著，
耶誕節可能飛揚的雪花。

又是許多年，
褪色的窗簾遙望，
南方怒放的梅花村，
而南方燕陣已突越節氣的圍困，
海浪正如四月的花草洶湧，
瘋狂的星空將以滿袖的頌歌，
放牧出慶賀的日神，
並揚起，
往事的那許多年。

1984.12於重慶歌樂山

Because of excessive boredom,

For many years, no one would be the first to look up

to watch the lights on the banks of the river.

Each of us carries so many unpleasant memories, and

meditating on the afternoon's bell has already diluted the red raindrops.

O, still so many years.

In fact, for many years,

The tracks were already closed.

The passage of sighing autumn leaves, and the eager eyes in the rain,

Only you forget warm cheeks in the autumn wind,

Crying, but hopelessly hoping, that

snowflakes may fall at Christmas.

And for many more years,

Faded curtains looking ahead, to

Plum Blossom Village in the south.

The southern swallows have flown across the siege of the season.

The ocean waves are rushing like the flowers and grass in April.

The crazy starry sky will be full of carols

Shepherding the sun god who celebrates.

So rise,

All you past years.

December 1984.   Chongqing Mount Gele
(English Trans. Matt Turner and Haiying Weng)

祖母軼事

祖祖已上高齡
昏濛濛的，
她扶倒園子一片青木
意外的靈通
她發明了拐杖

精巧像彩虹
祖祖萬萬沒有想到

老年人閒適多夢
一天，
屋頂上冒著炊煙
祖祖搓麻繩入了睡
夢像青煙繚繞
祖祖夢見一條口嗛珍珠的蛇
昂著頭，拍著水
向她遊來
祖祖翻身驚醒
發現麻繩纏了自己一頭

我出了一身的冷汗
這還是頭一次
祖祖如荷釋重

Anecdotes about Grandma

Granny is old
and disoriented,
She pressed down a green wood
By accidental inspiration
she invented a cane

Exquisite as a rainbow
Granny never expected that

Old people dream in their leisure
One day,
Smoke coming off the roof
Granny falls asleep while making a rope
Dreams like the curls of blue smoke
Granny dreamed of a snake with pearls in its mouth
Holding its head high, splashing the water
swimming to her
Granny rolled over and awoke
finding the rope tangled round her head

I broke out in a cold sweat
This was the first time
Granny floated like a lotus

鄉間的瓦房平易近人
祖祖衣食簡樸
清茶一杯，淡飯一碗
在黃昏的光輝裡，拂一拂長袖
祖祖身懷願望
發現穀倉又高了一層

還是農耕為本呀
祖祖布下了預言

清明時節
風中浮動一股祕密的香味
祖祖坐在木椅上
修養精深，
一隻博大的手蓋著紙錢
敲擊精緻的圖案
敲擊她失戀而寂寞的石頭
清明時節，祖祖削著蘿蔔
清晨的風掀動土壤
雨淅瀝而至
祖祖的淚水注滿了春祭的河流

The tiled houses of the countryside are friendly
Granny's lived a simple life
A cup of plain tea, a bowl of white rice
In the glow of twilight, brushing off sleeves
Granny has wishes, like
Finding the barn has raised up one more level

That farming is still the essence
Granny lays down prophesy

Qingming Festival-time
Secret fragrances floating in the wind
Granny sits on a wooden chair
cultivating profundities,
A broad hand covering the paper money
Knocking on the delicate patterns
Knocking on her lonely lovelorn stone
At Qingming-time, Granny's cutting a radish
The early morning wind rustles the soil
The whispering rain comes
Granny's tears fill the river of Spring sacrifice.

一九六三年
甘霖剛過
園子裡的枯木一片青綠
而那根拐杖
隨著祖祖一拋手
便永遠懸掛在天庭
精巧像彩虹

1987.9 於重慶歌樂山

1963

The sweet rain following drought, ended

The deadwood in the garden turns green

and that cane

Granny tossing it away

Hanging forever in heaven

Exquisite as a rainbow

September 1987. Chongqing Mount Gele
(English Trans. Matt Turner and Haiying Weng)

情人的頌詩

在節日
天空爽朗，霞光一片
情人身著綠葉
呼吸清晨的空氣
心臟在眼中跳動

蘋果圓圓的，綠綠的
懸在樹上，望風流

情人舉起雙手，天空在下
群鳥歌語，花園裡
釋放熱烈的氣息
在流泉之上，有
幾片白色的羽毛飛動，夢遠

木瓜切開，圓圓的腰身
瀉出淚眼的珍珠，花花閃光

正午時分，太陽好溫暖
情人一絲不掛，在
鮮紅的潮水中濯發
如透明的絲綢，情人
瞥見裸的糧食
長出茁壯的芽，夏的音樂

The Lover's Ode

At the festival
The sky is crisp and the sunlight is brilliant
The lover wears green leaves
Breathing in the morning air
The heart throbbing in the eyes

The apple is round, and green
Hanging from a tree, watching the air of romance

The lover raises her hands, and the sky hangs low
Flocks of birds singing in the garden
releasing hot breath
Above the flowing spring, there's
a few white feathers flying off, dreaming far away

Papaya cut open, a round waist
Tears like pearls pouring out, sparkling

By noon, the sun is warm
The lover is naked, and
washes her hair in the fresh red tide
Like transparent silk, the lover
glimpses the naked crops
growing strong buds, the music of summer

水撩動嫩莖，垂直的火苗
觸擊大地，天空，情人在飛翔

焰火升騰，夜色更燦爛
情人觀看星星，海的窗口
遊動成群的魚，童話般純真
船隻在浪中穿駛，她紅色的帆
聳入晴空，如一聲旗的召喚

情人啊，情人！快敲出心田的鼓聲吧
春天，節日，晴空，遠方：大家出發去遨遊

1995.2.14於香港中大

Water stirs the tender stem, a vertical flame
touches the earth, and the sky, the lover is flying

The fireworks rise up and the night grows light
The lover watches the stars, windows of the sea
Schools of fish swimming, a fairytale innocence
The ship sails among the waves, her red sail
hoisted into the clear sky, like the call of the flag

Lover o lover! Beat on the drum of the heart
The Spring, the festival, the clear sky, the distance:
 let's set out, and freely roam

February 14, 1995. CUHK
(English Trans. Matt Turner and Haiying Weng)

望梅八章

一

秋水怎麼能阻隔
江東暮雲的狂語？從娟月那邊
飛出的蟬噪，也會被今夜
竹屋裡的孤燈熄滅，霜氣濃重
空谷那邊躺著的俏美人
或許挪動她細軟的肩胛，從袖間
拋出苦思的……一縷白雲，一朵睡蓮
或夢見枝南枝北的九秋月色

二

你不能那樣，一想起往事
就悲傷，就搖落我日夜
思戀的芬芳，其實坦蕩孤憐
可能更體諒你高臥的厭倦
聽一聽馬兒的蹄音，去那年的努力
就會突然從你腳下促起，空澈並晶瑩
你殞落之日，便就竄起了滿天星星

三

風雨如晦的日子實在難熬
難道你還不寬恕我嗎？因我
在新年裡，撩拔不起對你的憐意

Eight Episodes of Looking at Plum Blossoms

1

How can autumn waters block the delirium
of dusk clouds on the east of the river? Cicada chirps
that fly over from the moon, only to be snuffed out
by the bamboo hut's lone light tonight, in the empty valley
thick with frosty air where a charming beauty lies
shifting her tender shoulder blade, tossing off
longing from her sleeves··· a wisp of white cloud, a water lily
or dreamt of autumn moonlight hanging over north and south branches

2

You shouldn't act like that, depressed as soon
as you think of the past, shaking off a fragrance
I yearn for day and night, but in fact a magnanimous love
might make more allowances for your reclusive weariness
listening to the hoofbeats, the exertion of going to that year
suddenly rushing up from beneath your feet, empty and clear
The day of your downfall, altered into a skyful of stars

3

The days of wind and rain are tough to live through
Do you still not forgive me? Because
in the New Year, affection for you can't be pulled up

損失一節枝頭就換回一程寂寞
我空手趕路，始終不見星星
想起那只棲落南枝的鳥兒，怎麼也禁不住
禁不住勾起你月光依依的鍾愛，以及
我許多年快淡忘對你的體諒與傾訴

四

下雪了，你說氣候真變幻無常
你在新年我家窗前停下，並抬頭
然此時我正履冰在外，你默語前行
留下一條我風雨裡溫暖多年的紅頭巾，自此
我不再有了親人，便寂寞深重，只在夜裡
盼望著鏡中的姣月，喚起林中
夕暮時水裡橫動的疏影

五

二月裡哀婉的糾纏，實在難以入眠
輾轉又反側，無不心事重重
難得的幾日清閒
也被你昨日早晨的霏雨驚醒
新加冕的皇后，搖著沉重的枝頭
款步依依，在醒來的清晨
走出山中那塊不安的土地

六

那座島嶼，活著時多麼年輕
在柳園裡，整日簪著信念的銅紋
有許多的日子，默念著昔日風中的雲裳

Losing one branch but bringing back a mile of solitude
I took to the road empty handed, never once seeing the stars
thinking of that bird perched on a south branch, I couldn't help
but evoke my moonlight affection for you, and
my multi-year faded memory of your cares and confessions

4

It's snowing, and you say the weather is mutable
At New Year's you stop by my window, raising your head
and right then I'm treading thin ice, you advancing in silence
to leave behind a red hood I warmed for years in wind and rain, and
I'll never have a lover again, lonesomeness deepening, only at night
will I look to the moon in the mirror, will I call on the scattered shadows
that shimmer on the water at dusk in the forest

5

The melancholy knots in February make it hard to sleep
turning and tossing, nothing but everything on my mind
A few days of clarity would be rare
and jolted awake yesterday morning by your drizzle
You newly coronated queen, swinging a heavy branch
dragging your slow feet, waking up in the morning
to walk out of that restless land in the mountains

6

That island, how young it was when alive
in the willow grove, hair pinned up with the copper veins of conviction
reading the past's cloud skirt in the wind to itself for many days

想見了乳燕撲打的翅膀，又開
晴空海水洶湧的蔚藍
希望迢遙，辛酸的往事日復一日
在黃昏，溢滿了柏舟的歸程

七

你與魚一同抵達，在黎明前來到我的陽臺上
我不清楚你到來的姿勢，那麼美麗多姿
只能想起那天晴空雲朵如雪，你話語親切
你等待過我並還會等待我多少次，我怎麼不銘記呢？
有關春天何時化雪，你又何時騎馬遠去
我怎麼不銘記呢？我高臥的俏君

八

你不會返顧那遠離你的枝頭，多麼高潔
而我長高的幼稚又是多麼的成熟
可能那遲到的聲音聽起來又是多麼像你
你在思慮，你終會畫出
你日夜夢寐的，破碎雪裡的
你的殞落與你的星星

1986.1於重慶歌樂山

wanting to see the young swallow's pounding wings, outspread
the surging blue of the sea water under clear sky
Hope seems remote, the sourness of the past day after day
in the dusk, overflowing with docked boats' homeward trips

7

You and the fish arrive together, reaching my balcony before dawn
I'm not sure about the gestures of your arrival, such beautiful poise
but can only recall the snowlike clouds that day, your words intimate
having waited for me and waiting again so many times, how could I forget?
As for when snow will be melted in spring, when will you ride off on a horse
how could I forget? My reclusive sovereign

8

I won't look back on that branch that has departed from you, so pristine
while my grown childishness turns out to be so mature
maybe those late noises sound so much like you
you in thought, you when finally painting
what you've dreamt of night and day, your downfall
and your stars in the shattered snow

January 1986. Chongqing Mount Gele
(English Trans. Lucas Klein)

惡男

一個男人剃光了頭
刮光了鬍鬚
灌著燒酒
啃著煙杆
整天拉扯武俠小說
走火入魔

這個男人暴虐自己的女人
每頓飯敲桌子
鼓動法力
他指令他的孩子
給他端酒杯

這個男人鬼迷心竅
用火澆灌花木
使它們含苞欲放
冬天枯水節
貓尿坐枯一朵花
這個男人整夜痛哭流涕

黑白電視的人物變了形
這個男人也變了形

一九八六年的一個晚秋
一對清白的小夫婦

A Vicious Man

A man shaves his head
scrapes off his whiskers
pours out some liquor
and gnaws on a pipe
and keeps nattering about martial arts fiction
walking through flames into devil

This man abuses his woman
bangs on the table at each meal
rouses supernatural powers
He commands his child
to bring him his glass

This man is truly possessed
Waters plants with fire
and brings them to the brink of blossoming
In the winter dry season
Cat urine dries out a flower
and this man sheds bitter tears at night

Characters on black-and-white TVs are twisted
This man is also distorted

In late autumn 1986
An honest young couple

被削光了頭
流放揚子江畔
他們習著出家人的謙和
閒事不管
荒唐事不做
讀古書
愛整潔
在陽光的石階上
摘下帽子
曬太陽
溫暖良心

1987.5 於重慶歌樂山下

| 輯二 | 望氣歌樂山 (1985–1995)　261
Cloud Divination on Mount Gele

have their hair shaved off
and are exiled to the banks of the Yangtze
They learn the meekness of votarists
have no interest in idle matters
commit no folly
study ancient texts
and adore tidiness
On sunlit flights of stone steps
they take off their hats
basking in the sun
warming their conscience

May 1987. Chongqing Mount Gele
(English Trans. Michael Day)

敲門之前

敲門之前
你會遭遇不測目光的侵襲
你會在樓梯旁換上防衛的衣裳
不停叫喚著自己的名字
你會想到年輕時你多豪邁強壯
曾掀起過海上重重驚濤駭浪
敲門之前的時刻
你寧靜的掌心裡會有風雲突起
你可能還會想起某些別的東西

那座村莊，桃花源裡的幽居
也會在你敲門之前，因你
畏懼的步劃，揚長而去
那江中船上，抱羞的琵琶
曾托起千百年鬱結的春心
也會以你突突的敲門聲
化為皖江嗚嗚的細水
你能想起的某些別的東西
在敲門前，會變成聲音向你逼近

那些故事，那些詩詞
你平時伴讀的好友
在你敲門之前，也不會
擔當任何角色，你更別企望
她會那麼仁慈而發善心

Before Knocking on Doors

Before knocking on a door
You'll be assaulted by unfathomable looks
You'll change into defensive clothes by the stairs
Constantly calling out your own name
You'll remember how bold and strong you were in youth
Having once raised terrifying waves
at that moment before knocking
In your calm palm a storm suddenly rises
You probably will remember something else

That village, a remote home in a land of peach blossoms
will also abruptly stalk off before you knock
Because of your fearful steps
On a boat on the river, a bashful pipa
once lifted long-stagnant hearts of spring
which with your burst of knocking will also
transform into the quiet murmur of the Yangtze
Other things you can remember
will become sounds pressing in on you before knocking

These stories, these poems
The good companion you used to study with
will also not play any role before you
knock on that door, you should hold out no hope
She'll be so kind and merciful

為你點起蠟燭，幫你
摘下掛在白楊樹上的賀年卡
在你敲門之前
她卻流水行歌，離你而去

就留下你孤單一人，我的好友
你可永遠不要忘懷呀
在你敲門之前
夜色清晰而溫柔
顫動的風鈴聲正從遠處轉來
比堅定的鑰匙
更使你從夢中驚醒

1984.12.15 於重慶歌樂山下

As to light a candle for you, help you

take down the New Year's card hanging in the poplar tree

Before you knock on that door

she's followed the river to sing her songs, away from you

Leaving you alone, my good friend

You must never forget

that before you knocked

The night was clear and tender

The return of the sounds of trembling windchimes far away

frightening you from your dreams more effectively

than an uncompromising key

December 15, 1984. Chongqing Mount Gele
(English Trans. Michael Day)

風拂過手掌

這是一個告別枯葉的時節
風拂過手掌，我感到了涼意
陽光照在水上，我的臉映在水裡
影子迷戀影子，如一棵開花的樹
如一顆結果的樹，月起月落
嚮往遙遠的夢境

今夜繁星遁離
我卻不能遠去，我要選擇道路
我要讓鳥兒捎信給我的愛人
晚潮如歸期
思念蕩著海濤，我卻不能啟航
海那邊升起的太陽，五瓣的金黃
那是否是伊人的臉龐，我眺望著她
我的伊人，絲綢般悠然又綿長

我不能消磨這無端的寂寞
群鳥遠飛天際，我卻匍匐在地上
我只能舉起雙手，把呼喚拋向空中
讓呢喃的燕子翔飛潤濕的江南

啊，親愛的伊人
聞聞那枚迷迭香
摸摸那枝掛在牆上的乾草花
翻翻幾頁捲曲的書稿

A Breeze Brushes over My Palm

This is a season to bid goodbye to dead leaves
A breeze brushes over my palm and I feel a chill
Sunlight shines on water, my face is reflected below
Shadow clings tight to shadow, like a tree in flower
Like a tree bearing fruit, the moon rises and falls
toward a distant dreamland

Tonight a sky full of stars flees
But I can't go far, I must choose a path
I want the birds to carry a message to my love
The evening tide like a return date

Yearning crashes with waves, but I can't set sail
The sun rising by the sea, five-petalled gold
is that the face of my love, I gaze on her
My love, carefree and lingering like silk

I cannot idle away this endless loneliness
Birds flock to the horizon, whereas I prostrate on the ground
I can only raise my hands and heave up my call
Let twittering swallows soar over a soaking Southland

Ah, my dear
Smell the rosemary
Touch the hay flower on the wall
Flip the curling pages of manuscripts

聽聽唱盤機轉動的舊曲
晚潮正滿過天際線
柔情將會如期而至

　　　　　　　　　　　1988.11.15 於北大

Listen to an old tune on the record player

The evening tide has just risen past the horizon

Tenderness will arrive in its own time

November 15, 1988. Beida
(English Trans. Michael Day)

贈友

春光裡
與老朋友端坐
心心相印
我們血紅的細胞
在雨水中點種
讓未來的日子豐盛

這是道路最後的時刻
所有的植物腐化
所有的糧食腐化
所有的花朵腐化
為了美麗的雨水
在未來的鄉土裡
溢出芬芳的果實

這是冬日最後的夜晚
我飄泊在外，
寒風簌簌
雪花紛揚
我知心的友人捎來了
溫暖的酒
光的焰火
一個盛大的節日從天而至

1991.1.10 於北大

For a Friend

In the spring light
Sitting with an old friend
Hearts alike
Our blood red cells
Planting seeds in the rain
For enriching future days

This is the last moment of this path
All plants decay
All grain rots
All flowers fade
For the pretty rain
In a future native land
to overflow with fragrant fruit

This is the last night of winter
I wander outside,
A cold wind soughs
Snowflakes flutter
My intimate friend brings
warm wine
bright fireworks
a great festival arrives from the sky

January 10, 1991. Beida
(English Trans. Michael Day)

凌晨斷章

凌晨很清涼
風兒怎麼也不說話
是雨點？打在芭蕉葉上
窗外彷彿有聲音
這很使人憂傷
指尖不聽使喚
好像有人叩門
好像有腳步聲逼近
牆上白熾燈閃爍不定
欲走？欲進？
凌晨的鳥頭夾在樹葉間
薄霧中卻露出警覺的眼神

不說你也清楚
比如正面看人
你就孤立萬分
不過這還難言斷定
但路上講的那程故事
卻早已滑進了後花園
正混合著滴落的花朵
記起又忘記

Fragments before Dawn

Early mornings are very refreshing
How does the wind not speak?
Is it raindrop hitting the plantain leaves?
There seems to be a sound outside the window
This makes one sad
Fingertips don't obey commands
It seems somebody knocks
It seems footsteps draw near
An incandescent wall-lamp flickers
A desire to go? To come in?
The heads of pre-dawn birds are wedged among tree leaves
and watchful eyes revealed in a mist

You know without it being said
As if looking at somebody straight on
You're isolated to an extreme
Yet it's still hard to judge
But the story told on the way
Long ago slipped into the back garden
and is mingling with the dripping flowers
Remembered then forgotten

記憶猶新的東西實在不會深刻
就像兩人之間拉開的距離
不那麼引人注意
昨天船隻駛過的海濤
而今又複歸平靜
你說水手能否記起
義大利商船何時掛上中國彩旗
而你一生崇拜的頭像
瞬間就便變成了貓頭玩具

不說你也清楚
記憶猶新的東西實在容易忘記
風兒日漸急促
是雨點？打在芭蕉葉上
窗外確實有了聲音
這怎麼不使人緊張
雖說塔上又響起了鐘聲
但是凌晨依然很清涼

1985.2.5 於重慶歌樂山下

Things remembered afresh actually can't go deep
Just like the distance opened between two people
Doesn't attract much attention
The waves the ship navigated yesterday
are calm again today
You speak of whether a sailor can remember
when Italian trading ships hung Chinese bunting
and the portrait you've worshipped all your life
instantly becomes the head of a toy cat

You know without it being said
Things remembered afresh are actually easily forgotten
The wind grows more urgent day by day
Is it raindrop hitting the plantain leaves?
There is definitely a sound outside the window
How does this not make you tense?
Though they say the tower bell tolls again
Dawn is still very refreshing

February 5, 1985. Chongqing Mount Gele
(English Trans. Michael Day)

贈言

在生命最困難的時候，
喚醒些美好而具體的事物——
一些迷人而難忘的書本，
幾段動情的文字（你自己寫的），
幾種撫舊的手工製品（你親手做的），
二，三條常獨步的小路，
二，三種常吃的熱帶水果……

在那裡，只有秩序和美麗，
只有溫馨，安寧和逍遙。

好朋友，
難得生存，更難得重聚
在生命最窒息的時候，
奔向些美好而陌生的地方——
一座綠色蔥蘢的山巒，
一塊莊稼燦爛的田野，
一條白雲映照下的小溪，
一線海鷗嬉戲的沙灘……

那裡是一座美好而芬芳的花園，
住進去吧，好朋友，
人生在世，
至少敢做一次烏托邦者，
在生命最困惑的時候，

To A Departing Friend

When life comes to its most difficult moment,
conjure up some beautiful and concrete things—
Some amazing and unforgettable books,
Some paragraphs of touching words（written by yourself）,
Some kinds of worn-out handicrafts（made by yourself）,
Two or three trails where you often walk alone,
Two or three tropical fruits which you often love eating…..

There lies only order and beauty,
Only warmth, peace and leisure.

My good friend,
It is tough to live on, even harder to have a reunion.
When life is in the most suffocating moment
Let us run towards those beautiful and strange places —
A greenish and luxuriant mountain,
A field with shining crops,
A brook reflecting the white clouds above,
A beach with frolicing seagulls……

That is a beautiful and fragrant garden,
Move into it, my friend,
Live in this world,
You should dare to be a utopian at least once,
When life comes to its most perplexing moment,

某些豪邁的壯舉，
更令你終身難忘。

我們同是天底下飄動的羽毛，
重逢的日子肯定不會太遙遠，
只是在告別去舊的一剎那，
說些溫熱的話，
講些神奇的故事，
好在未來重聚的日子裡，
我們才有記憶喚起。

1992.6.14 於重慶歌樂山

Some heroic behaviors,

will immortalize your life.

We are all feathers drifting under the sky,

The date for reunion won't be too far.

At this moment of farewell,

We'll have a warm chat,

share some legendary stories,

so that when we meet again,

We can have good memory to recall.

June 14, 1992. Chongqing Mount Gele
(English Trans. Feng Yi)

梨花與影子

為什麼那個溺死在兩個小河間的女孩
不像所有的船隻飄向大海？

——《我想知道》阿雷桑德利（西班牙）

不要遲疑，
快逃走吧，
圓圓的水果
將搗碎你的面容；
把雙腳抬起來，
用雙手捂著雙眼，
也許從手指的漏縫中
瞥見梨花微開的雪亮；
也許僅一次霜打
該不會凍壞你紅潤的清香；
水銀柱一般的影子
驅使你趕快逃走，
「趕快逃走」
「快——快、快啊！」

何物將從你那裡潛逃，
你的面容，如雨後的花瓣。
我們尾隨著那條長長的影子
溜進了風信子與茴香的粉紅帶上，

Pear Flowers and Shadow

Why doesn't the little girl who drowned herself between the two rivers
flow into the ocean as all the ships do?

——Vicente Aleixandre (Spain), "*I Want to Know*"

Don't hesitate,
Flee away fast,
Roundish fruit,
will smash your face.
Lift up your feet,
Cover your eyes with both hands,
Perhaps through the gaps of your fingers,
Glimpse the faint whiteness of pear blossoms;
Perhaps only one hit by frost
will not frostbite your ruddy fragrant scent;
A mercury-like shadow
drives you to flee away fast.
"Flee away fast"
"Fast------Fast, Fast!"

What will flee away from you?
Your face is like petals after rain.
We follow that long shadow
sneaking into the pinkish ribbon of hyacinths and fennels,

臥倒，枕著老虎噴火的夢，
暈眩，痙攣，喘息，
這些舉動便阻止了我們的傾聽——
海藻蕩浪急促的呼吸，
梨花擠壓煩躁的騷動；
「這一切不是夢吧？」
「說也是，我們總會失眠的」
「這你也知道？」
「那該不會記錯吧！」
「嗯，——那個……」

我們終於逃走了，
「逃走了！」
我們總會逃走的，
無論是睡眠還是清醒，
在你數學般精確的記憶中
一個影子在梨花樹下卷著碎瓣，
一次致命的危機正卷湧街區。

「媽呀！這命太……」
「難道老虎不也是很痛苦嗎？」
「哎，梨花呀，梨……花……」
「OUUuu——OUUuu——OUUuu——」
我們都不必焦慮，

lying down, dreamed of tiger's spitting fire,

Spin, lurch, gasp,

These acts prevent us from listening—

The gasp of seaweeds in turbulent waves

The irritating fury of the crushing pear petals

"Is this all a dream?"

"It is said so. We are always insomniac"

"You even know this?"

"It cannot be wrong!"

"Hum,— that⋯."

We finally flee away

"Fled away!"

We will always succeed in fleeing,

No matter whether we are asleep or awake,

In your memory of mathematical accuracy,

A shadow is stranding up crushed petals under a pear tree,

A deadly crisis is sweeping the streets.

"Gosh! This life is too⋯."

"Isn't the tiger also in pain?"

"Ouch, pear flowers, pear⋯ flowers⋯."

"OUUuu— OUUuu— OUUuu—"

We shouldn't be anxious

既然年輕的水手已將手中
雪白的泡沫潑灑了你，
既然昨晚的波濤早已
騷擾你熟睡的帳篷；
既然早春的哨音飄散了
你銀霜似的記憶；
那一切妄想皆成定局，
命運註定了你隕落的星辰。

「這該怎麼辦呀？」
「……EHH」
「我要要，我想要，」
「那山中的藤樹該……」
「不……不……不！」
「你該到海邊去！」
「我要，這不是真的，」
「我要——我要——我想要——-我！」

昨夜的涼風驚擾了你的睡意，
這一切都是真的，
反正水果店行將關門，
蝸牛不會再爬上山崗；
六點鐘的烏鴉將

Since the young sailor has already splashed
white foams from his hand over you,
Since last night's roaring wave has already disrupted
the tent of your sound sleep
Since the early spring's whistle has already faded away
your memory of silver frost
All delusions are doomed.
Fate has dictated you are a fallen star

"What should we do?"
"···.EHH"
"I want, want, I want to"
"The rattan tree in the mountain will···."
"No··· no···no!"
"You should go to the sea!"
"I want, but can't be this unreal,"
"I want—I want—I want—I!"

Last night's chilly breeze stirs your sleep,
All that happens is real,
After all the fruit store will be closed,
Snails won't climb up the hill anymore;
Crows at six o'clock in the evening will

窒息你體內的呼吸；
趁著晨霜尚未挪近，
讓我們逃走吧！
什麼都從你那裡逃走，
你的，我的，
枯藤，老樹，
藍天，白雲，
正朝著腥紅的背影退移。

1985.3.25於重慶歌樂山下

suffocate the breath inside your body;

As the morning frost is not spreading near,

Let us flee away!

All will flee away from you,

Yours, mine,

Withered vines, old trees,

Blue sky, white cloud

Are retreating from the crimson shadow from behind.

March 25, 1985. Chongqing Mount Gele
(English Trans. Feng Yi)

冬晚遐思

那冬晚風中，
輪轉的木葉，宛如
一頁珠算似的日曆，
在卷點陶罐依稀的波紋。

田野裡，
劃出馬鞭的車痕，
風向標扭向逶迤的江晚；
天空，
烏鴉飛過，
我們不能再等。

比如努力與艱辛，
比如美麗與青春；
其實流年返顧，不如
拂手寒棹，風荷搖櫓
把酒清點孤燈。

小徑旁，
攀折一絮曉霜的煙柳，
梳織成一個蘋果似的溜圓，
然後刻下乳燕溫暖的剪影，
舉手加額，
拋向灰白如面頰的長江，
隨江水，尋找出口的方向。

1984.12.8 於歌樂山下

Reveries on a Winter's Evening

In the winter evening wind,
gyrating leaves and branches, like
an abacus page of a calendar,
punctuating the illusive corrugations on pottery.

In the fields,
traces of vehicles spreading out horsewhips,
weather vanes twist towards a winding river evening;
in the sky,
blackbirds fly by,
we can wait no more.

For instance, great effort and hardship,
beauty and youth;
but actually, looking back on years past is not as good as
dismissing the cold with a wave of a hand, the swaying of lotus in the wind
clears a bit of the wine off a solitary lamp.

Beside the footpath,
pull down a wispy spray of willow in the dawn frost,
weave it into a circle like an apple,
then cut out the warm silhouettes of young swallows,
raise your hands to your forehead,
toss them toward the Yangtze white as a cheek,
follow the water, search out the direction to its mouth.

December 8, 1984. Chongqing Mount Gele
(English Trans. Michael Day)

六月，江風拂面

六月，
那縺褓中鏗亮的紐扣
望著江上拉長的汽笛
　　　　　　　　叩首；

調皮的兩雙小手，
熄滅了微溫的煙蒂，
驚飛了夢中的小蜻蜓，
彩飛中的金黃色蝴蝶，
沙灘上急促的濕潤呼吸。

六月就是這樣，但並非如此，
就這樣，六月的微雨，
洗滌了路上的塵土，
潑響了孩子們的歡笑，
竄入草叢中
找尋手帕裡遺忘的典故。

六月的荊棘，
刺破我滿身塵封的肌膚，
讓貪婪的光吮吸我滾燙的血；
只為了那只山間歡躍的小鹿，
拂一手紅葉的柔光，向你奔來
追逐，
蒲公英唱起那哀傷的訣別之歌。

June, River Breeze Rustles By My Face

June,
the shining button in the cradle
glances at the long steam whistle

                Kowtowing;

Two pair of little naughty hands,
extinguish a tepid cigarette's butt,
flush a little dragonfly in a dream,
Golden butterfly in its colorful flight,
Rasping breaths of moisture on the beach.

Such is happening in June, but not just this,
In this, June's drizzles,
Cleanse the dirt on the road,
Stir up the joys of the children,
and jump into the grass,
looking for the forgotten allusions in a handkerchief.

June's thorns,
stab my dust-covered skin,
Allow greedy lights to suck my boiling blood;
Only for the joyous dancing fawn in the mountain,
Fondle a handful gentle light of red leaves, and run towards you
Chasing,
The sorrowful song of farewell the dandelion starts to sing.

六月啊！
你說你很任性，
任性得黑暗因你害怕，
任性得寒冬因你消隱；
你呀，這麼任性，
只為了鳥鳴在你的碧潭裡，
　　　　　　　　搗碎，
你才說那只是任性的天真，
　　　　　　　　　　只是
為了阻止海浪的翻滾，
風的謀殺，
霧的驕橫。

六月，
兩股跌打的潛流，
在「嘩啦啦」地演習。

把我琥珀色的記憶，六月
用你火熱的紫光焊合吧！
搗碎在你氤氳的花蕊裡，
笛管的音韻，
從深林深處溢出，飄散。
那位雅典的美少女
舉起她螢火蟲的斷臂，
把披散的黑髮
溫柔地向松濤潑灑。

Ah, June!
You say you are indulgent,
So indulgent that darkness is scared of you,
So indulgent that cold winter retreats from you,
You, how can you be so indulgent?
For the singing of birds in your green pool,
                              Crushed apart,
You say that is just indulgent childishness,
                              Only
For preventing waves from rolling and eddying
The wind's murder,
The mist's arrogance.

June,
Two mingled and colliding undercurrents,
are performing a drill run of "Hua-la-la."

June, seams my amber memory
with your fiery purple lights!
Stamp crushes in your misty stamen and pistil,
The melody of a pipe,
overflowing from the deep forest, drifting away.
That graceful beautiful girl
lifts up her broken arm of fireflies,
hanging down her dark hair
gently splashes towards the waves of pine trees.

六月啊，我心愛的六月，
可愛啊！
微風中那飄起的紅色衣裙
　　　　　跳躍著
　　　　　　奔
　　　　　　跑
　　　　　　著
　　　　　　延伸著
她瘋狂的翱翔，誘惑的生長
只為了一個願望
　　　　　　一
　　　　　　個
　　　　　企望……
只完成一個方向，一次眺望。

六月要有光，就有光，
魚鱗滑動的姿勢，
牽引著一輪青綠的月亮，
在水草間，
倘佯……
你說就讓她走向湖岸，
不在返回，
直至遺忘；
六月有暴漲的琴弦，
在懸崖的漏縫裡，
鳴響；
六月有戲水的木槳，
在柳枝的漩渦裡，

Ah, June, my adorable June,

How adorable!

The red dress floating up in the breeze

        hopping

           run

             n

           ing

        stretching

She soars wildly, and flourishes alluringly

For only one single wish

          one

       single

    yearning

For one single direction, one single overlooking.

June wants lights, and it has lights,

The gesture of the gliding fish scales

pulls a greenish moon,

Among the waterweeds,

strolling and roaming······

You say: let her go to the lakeside,

and have no return,

Until forgetting;

June has her surging chords,

in the crevice of cliffs,

sounding;

June has her paddling oars,

In the swirls of willow branches,

蕩漾；
有港口的微波，
正擁抱，
含情晚歸的魚郎；
有田埂上的桑樹，
在吻別，
灑淚西去的夕陽。

六月，
那射出的響箭，
絷進橡樹動脈裡。

天空，
放飛著一個傲慢的紙鷂，
孩子們如此天真，
竟相信用一根細細的藍線，
就可以使天空與大地傾談；
你來了，帶著雪鄉的記憶，
從報紙的碎屑裡，
你拾到一條驚人的消息，
從此，天空不再蔚藍，
風箏也不在攀登，
我也不再幻想。

不再懷疑，
薄霧裡綠葉中，
忽閃忽現的祕密，
　　　　忽

rowing;

June spreads the ripples at ports,

embracing,

fishermen returning late from the sea;

June has mulberry trees on the ridges,

kissing farewell to

tearful Sun going down to the West.

June,

The arrows are shot with whistling,

and punctured in the arteries of oaks.

In the sky,

An arrogant paper kite is soaring,

Children are so naïve

that they believe a thin blue thread

can make the sky and the earth converse;

You come with the memory of snow country.

From the scrapes of newspaper,

You find a piece of startling news,

From then on , the sky is no longer blue,

The kite no longer climbs up,

and I dream no more.

No longer do I suspect,

In the mist on the leaves,

Those flickering secrets,

Fli

　　　　　　　閃
　　　　忽
　　　　　　現的
等你用秋天的豔陽去破譯。
啊！我爽快的六月，
爽快的眼睫上那
忽
　　　　閃
　　　　　　　忽
　　　　　　　　　　現的
淡紫色的詭笑。

雲雀啄破了夜的煩悶，
火球，
豌豆花在搖曳中旋轉，
窗臺上茉莉花吐出的香圈，
　　　　　　　一圈
　　　　　　　　圈圈
紫葡萄瑩燈邊的淚痕，
　　　　　　一陣
　　　　　　　　陣陣
葡萄樹傳來露珠自殺的哭聲，
　　　　　　一陣陣
　　　　　　很低

　　　　　一聲聲
　　　　　很沉
…… …… ……

               ck

         er

                ing

Waiting for you to be decoded with the bright sun in autumn.

Ah! My refreshing and enlightening June,

Your enticing eyelashes are with

Fli

    ck

      er

            ing

Enchanting lavender smiles

Larks peck into the boredom of night,

Fire balls,

Pea flowers swirl in their swaying dance,

Jasmine flowers on the windowsill blow circles of fragrance,

                     one circle

                  circles of circles

Traces of tears on the glistening purple grapes lights

                     A crying

                  One and another

Suicidal cries were heard from the dews on the grape trees

                        cries

                    very low cries

                    one cry and two

                    very low crying

....

六月，
點燃了我那瀑布沖熄的燈，
在我飢餓的深林裡前行。

祝福吧，六月，
我將在你熾熱的照耀下，
去尋找夏天的綠蔭；
為了甜蜜的果醬，
讓我們越過清晨的柵欄，
去托起那顆正午的純心。

　　　　　　　　　　1984.6.23 於重慶歌樂山下

June,

Light my lights which have been extinguished by waterfall,

Advance forward in my starving forest.

Best wishes for you, June,

In your blazing sunshine, I will

start to look for shades in summer;

For the sweet jam,

Let us cross over the morning's fence,

to pick up the pure heart of the noon.

June 23, 1984. Chongqing Mount Gele
(English Trans. Feng Yi)

四月遊春

以刺破視窗的目光，
你膽怯地伸縮了
我心焦的造訪。
不再是因為卷起赤腿的田埂，
阻截了你舒卷的發波，
在麥尖突圍的擠壓中；
不再是因為雨打芭蕉的驚歎，
刺傷了你冰浪的彈指，
在脊背的陽臺上延伸。

四月，那麼多旋轉的色彩，
正困擾著地面塵土的窺望。

不只是一次飛越，
就能使蜻蜓展翅飛揚，
不只是一次偷渡，
就能突破港口的設防，
不只是一陣深夜的春雷，
就能炸出走廊空蕩的迴響，
不只是一次突圍，
就能制止群鳥紛紛的陣亡。

哎，就為了一個中心，
太陽蒙著光頭撫摸月亮，
蜘蛛欲從房間的窗沿，

Spring Outing in April

From my look that penetrates the window,
You timorously stretch out and draw back
my anxious visit.
Not for the ridge of the field, where you roll up your pants,
cuts the rolling waves of curly hair,
Among the crushing tips of wheat ears for the breakout;
Not for the shocks at the rain drops on banana leaves,
stab your icy waves of flipping fingers,
stretching out on the back of the balcony.

April, there are so many swirling colors,
disturbing the peeps of dirt on the ground.

Not by one single leap,
can make a dragonfly soar in the air;
Not by one time stowaway,
can the fortification at the port be broken;
Not by one single spring thunder at night,
can blast the echoes in the hollow corridor;
Not by one sole breaking away from a siege,
can stop flocks of birds from being killed.

Alas, just for the sake of a center,
The sun covers his bald head to caress the moon;
From the windowsill in the room, Spiders

掙脫玻璃透明的背光。
四月，微卷的樹葉，
汗珠在白白地死去。

春日霍霍，瀑布滑動，
漣漪的落櫻棄甲而逃；
岩石邊，
連衣裙掃蕩嫩唇的金盞花，
晶瑩的晨露鍍滿了一匹布紋，
「春去尚早！」

春去尚早啊！
木舟從山中滑出
沿著方格與布紋擦出的方向。

　　　　　　　　　　　　1985.5.26 重慶歌樂山下

want to break from the transparent backlight of the glass.

April, on your slightly curled leaves,

drops of sweat are dying for nothing.

Flickering spring, gliding waterfall,

Rippling fallen cherry blossoms drop their armors and flee;

Beside the rocks,

The skirt sweeps the tender lips of marigold flowers,

Glistening morning dewsrops gild a piece of colored cloth,

"Too early for spring to pass away!"

Too early for spring to pass away!

Wooden boat rows through the mountain,

along the direction traced by the square and the lines of skirt.

May 26, 1985. Chongqing Mount Gele
(English Trans. Feng Yi)

青春流光

1981-1984

Flashes of Youth

小鎮晚景

你倚門觀天，街上空無一人
彷彿有東西掉下，誰也沒來拾起
天氣陰晦，碎雨拍打玻璃窗
收音機開響，始終播不出新聞
茶一直沒來，卻又不敢去詢問
聽說今夜風暴將起，誰也沒去關門
有人匆匆離去，似乎夜色將近
小孩子回屋，門哐當一聲
母親生火，炊煙彌漫
街上傳來急促的車輛聲
收工的時間到了

1983.4.28 於新場

Evening Scene in a Small Town

Leaning against the door, you watch the sky, streets are empty

As if something falls down from the sky, but nobody picks it up

The weather is gloomy, and the splattering rain knocks on the windows

The radio is turned on, but no news is being aired

The tea is still not served, but I dare not go to ask

I hear that a storm will strike this town tonight, yet nobody closes the door

Some people are leaving hurriedly, and when the night is approaching

Children are back home, and the door is closed with a bang

Mother makes fire, and cooking smoke rises

Pressing noises of vehicles are heard from the street

It's time to knock off

April 28, 1983. New Market Town
(English Trans. Feng Yi)

燈亮著

燈，閃亮著
在表達一種情緒
銅鐘嗡鳴
在傳播一陣音響

燃燒著，你的光
毀滅了陰影的企望
驅跑了小孩子的貓藏
遁入狂野流浪

不是為了別的
亮著，只為亮著
當蔓藤纏死掙扎的時辰
燧人氏便潑灑星雲

於是，洪荒隆起綠色的脊背
人間就流傳著你的童話
不是為了別的，亮晶晶
岩石上杜鵑銜來一枚血紅花

燈，亮著，只是為了亮著
由此黑暗將不再挪近
星空將屬於無憂的童年
在火柴尖上呼鳴

1983.3.16於重慶歌樂山下

The Light's On

The light is glittering
expressing its emotion
The copper clock is buzzing
spreading a burst of its klang

Burning, your light
destroys the shadow's motive
drives the child's game away
retreats to wandering the land

Not for any other reason
Lighting only for lighting's sake
When vines are entangled in struggle
the fire inventor douses stars and clouds

So, the primal world hunches its green back
Your legend has spread among men
Glittering, not for any other reason
On the rock a cuckoo brings a bloody red flower

The light shines only for shining's sake
Ever since, darkness can no longer approach
The starry sky will belong to a carefree childhood
puffing up on the matchtip

March 16, 1983. Chongqing Mount Gele
(English Trans. Matt Turner and Haiying Weng)

暗示

你說枯葦中流旋的暈暈淡綠，
把凝滯從冬的指甲上削離；
你說雨中微顫的紅色衣裙，
正啄破笛管中發寒的寂靜；

葡萄閃亮的微紫，
蘋果流汁的痛惜，
還有瞳仁般的花格襯衫；
這一切溫柔的衝擊，
你說都需要用心去破譯。

夕陽，
在把西邊盼離，
你說讓我們一道，
乘一葉風帆把黎明托起。

1983.11.22 於重慶歌樂山下

Suggestions

You say light green circling among the dry reeds,
cuts stagnation from the fingernails of winter;
You say the red dress trembling in the rain,
pecks through cold stillness emanating from the flute.

Grapes sparkle a little with purpleness,
The juicing regret from the apple,
and the pupil-like checkered shirt.
With all this gentle pushing,
You say they all need to be deciphered with care.

The setting sun,
is departing into the west,
You say let us go,
and ride a sail to lift up the dawn.

November 22, 1983. Chongqing Mount Gele
(English Trans. Matt Turner and Haiying Weng)

啊，故鄉！一翔閃光的彩羽
——在群星閃爍的天幕上我聽見一群飛鶴在放歌

一宗清澈的流水，
呼吸著田野的甜溫，
一樽白塔的靚影，
默蕩著我鄉思的釀醞。

啊，故鄉！我心中蔚藍的瞳仁。

我哼著童年的夢，
追逐著玉米葉上綠絲輕吟的恬靜；
我踏著故鄉彎曲折折的石徑，
推算著故鄉遠去而褪色的年輪；
我用粗糲而堅韌的犁耙，
耕尋著故鄉失落而延長的青春；
我回眸望著被風沙侵蝕成怪額的沙岸，
輕輕地聆聽著河水粼粼波光的音韻。

啊，故鄉！我靈魂的歸宿，
　　　　　我熱戀的蘊藏。

我深吸著隨風飄飄的穀香，
佇立在粒粒金輝噴發的雲朵上，
遠望見一片閃光的彩羽，
　　　　馱著血凝的希翼，

O! Hometown! A Flash of Colorful Wings
——On the vault with flickering constellations
I heard a flock of cranes singing loudly

A clear-flowing stream,
breathing the sweet air of the field,
The grand shadow of a pagoda,
rippling my growing homesickness.

O! Hometown! The azure pupil in my heart.

I hummed my childhood dream,
chasing the tranquility of corn's green silken leaves.
Treading the winds and folds of my hometown's cobble trails,
I calculate my hometown's fading growth rings.
I use a rough, firm plow,
to plow my hometown's lost, prolonged youth.
I glance back at the strange sandbank eroded in the wind,
listening to the shimmering melody of the crystalline water.

O! Hometown! The lodging of my soul,
         The reserves for my passions.

I inhale the scent of grains riding on the wind,
Standing on clouds as golden particles erupt,
I see a flash of colorful wings in the distance,
         Driving the clotted wings of hope,

盈盈地，盈盈地，
　　　飛翔……

啊！這一片旋飛的彩羽，
　　潛寄著清麗的流雲，
似雄鷹翱騁蒼穹的力臂，
她裝載了騰飛的強度，
她也將爆射出這力度的光芒。

升騰吧！這甘甜的富強與發寒的貧窮的鏖戰，
　　　這歡樂與痛苦的較量；
攀登吧！我的彩色的翔羽，
　　　翔羽是我飛奔的故鄉。

　　　　　　　　　1982.3.25於重慶歌樂山下

Graceful, graceful
Flight···.

O! This swirling of colorful wings,
Submerging exquisite clouds,
Like the strong legs of the soaring eagle
She's loaded with the strength of flight,
and she's going to blast its radiance out.

Arise! The battle between sweet wealth and chilling poverty,
The contest between joy and pain.
Climb up! My colorful, soaring wings,
For soaring wings are my hometown in flight.

March 25, 1983. Chongqing Mount Gele
(English Trans. Matt Turner and Haiying Weng)

夜讀

　　　皎潔的月光，
　流放在靜靜的窗紗上，
　　　飛螢的夜色，
　悄悄地從屋頂上滑翔。

　　　耐心地等著，
　月光浸映的沙灘，
　　　渴望著貝殼，
　饋贈的片片璀璨。

思緒，
抖開跳躍的金絲線，
行吟者的步劃，
大海鼓滿的風帆。

神奇的迷宮，
在這裡得到發現，
沙灘包含的金粒，
在這裡得到篩選。

　　　　　　　　　　　1982.4於重慶歌樂山下

Reading At Night

Pure moonlight,
overflows on the window screen,
Night fireflies
silently glide off the roof.

Waiting patiently,
The beach immersed in moonlight.
Yearning for a shell,
Endowed with rays of brilliance.

Thoughts
shake off bouncing golden silk threads,
The troubadour's singing steps,
like the full sails of the sea.

A mystical labyrinth
is discovered here.
The grains of gold in the beach
are miraculously sifted here.

April, 1982. Chongqing Mount Gele
(English Trans. Matt Turner and Haiying Weng)

南泉春遊

尋著春天的弦音，
踏著嫩葉的銀鈴，
拉著袖口的旋風，
來到溫泉池邊。

我微笑，向
花蕊裡甜蜜的春雨，
搖醒的蝴蝶花瓣，
抽芽的綠樹與湛藍的天。

碧池掛著相思的垂柳，
春雨洗滌的小石徑，
樹上鳥兒婉轉的歌鳴，
漂浮在湖中漣漪的脆笑。

遊人像青青綠草，
露出殷勤的笑靨，
吮吸暖暖的陽光，
執希冀跨入明朝。

1982.3.25 於重慶南泉

Spring Trip to the Southern Spring

Tracing Spring's melody,
Stepping on the silver bells of young leaves,
Pulling at the cyclone at the cuff,
I arrive at the hot spring.

I beam, towards
the sweet Spring dew on the pistil,
The iris petal that has just awoken,
The sprouting green tree and azure sky.

The lovesick willows hang over the green pond,
The stone path washed by the Spring rain,
The soft song of the bird in the tree,
A crisp smile ripples across the lake.

The visitors are like green grass,
Radiating gracious smiles,
Suckling the warm sunshine,
And with hope, stepping into tomorrow.

March 25, 1982. Chongqing Southern Spring
(English Trans. Matt Turner and Haiying Weng)

我與土地

我從洪水淹沒過的土地上，
拾起一杯黑土，
我從黑土的紋理上，
覓見了人類生存的基因。

我用汗水澆灌鮮綠的田野，
我用鋤頭掘出春天的馨香，
我用鐮刀收割秋天的金黃，
我用犁鏵耕耘晨露的榮光。

我只知道農民對土地的深情，
我只知道勤勞才能掀開滾滾麥浪，
我只知道珍愛黑魆魆的熱土，
我只知道開墾沉睡的荒涼。

清新，泥土輻射的甘甜，
靜雅，河水蕩漾的波紋。

我帶著饑渴的嚮往，
耕耘那片溢血的黑土，
我堅信自己的耕耘，
必將是一份至福的收成。

> 1982.11 於重慶歌樂山下

The Land and Me

From the floodlands,

I pick up a cup of black earth,

From the veins of the black earth,

I find the gene for mankind's survival.

I use sweat to irrigate the fresh green fields,

I use a hoe to till Spring's fragrance,

I use a scythe to reap Autumn's gold,

I use a plough to till the glory of the morning dew.

I only know the farmer's deep love of the land,

I only know that diligence opens the waves of wheat,

I only know to cherish the fertile black soil,

I only know to cultivate the sleeping barrenness.

Fresh, sweetness spreading in the soil,

Elegance, ripples undulating in the river.

With my thirsty longing,

I am plowing the bloody black soil,

I have conviction that my tillage,

will reap a bountiful harvest.

November 1982. Chongqing Mount Gele
(English Trans. Matt Turner and Haiying Weng)

在深林的搖籃裡

我躺在綠色的深林裡，
　躺在鬆軟的草地上，
婆娑的金色陽光，
　在嫩草尖上閃亮。

美妙的交響曲，
飄過這幽綠色的深林，
我輕沐著松風的奏鳴，
靈魂裡滾動著自然的體溫。

小草隨著微風搖動，
綠葉鍍上清亮的金黃，
我躺在這綠色的搖籃裡呀！
伴著醉人的春曲，輕輕地，
輕輕地搖盪。。。

攬著美好的憧憬，
在這生機勃勃的海洋裡倘佯，
吻著清輝的瑩光，
滿懷激情，舒爽地哼唱。

1982.4於重慶歌樂山下

In the Cradle of the Deep Forest

I lay in the green forest,
   Lay in the soft grasses,
The dancing golden sunlight,
shines on the young grasstips.

A wonderful symphony,
drifts through the dark green forest,
I bathe in the pine's soughing sonata,
Nature's energy roiling in my soul.

Little grasses sway with the breeze,
Green leaves plated in bright gold,
I'm lying in this green cradle!
I gently sway to Spring's intoxicating song,
Slowly, slowly rolling······

Upholding this beautiful hope,
Strolling in the vigorous ocean,
Kissing the clear light,
In a flux of exuberance I hum.

April 1982. Chongqing Mount Gele
(English Trans. Matt Turner and Haiying Weng)

高樓瞭望

高速穿梭的電流，
驅碎了昏昏欲睡的夜色，
月光灑下的破碎的花邊，
鑲嵌在華燈輝映的牆面。

電焊璀璨的閃爍，
編織一個夜的彩屏，
星輝的饋贈，
照亮了大廈未來的精靈。

凝慮的眉，
橫江的思緒，
扇扇窗口的憧憬，
從大廈的體溫裡延伸。

宿著星夜，伴著黎明，
為了明天的歡笑，
他們用大廈鼓肌的臂，
擔負起共和國明朝的使命。

1982.12.5於重慶歌樂山下

Tower Gazing

The current that swiftly shuttles by,
dislodges the night's somnolence,
The tattered lace that moonlight pours down,
inlaid in the lantern's reflections on the wall.

Twinkling flash of the welding torch,
weaves the colorful screen of the night,
The emanations of starlight,
illumine the tower's future spirit.

Furrowed brow,
Thoughts traversing rivers,
The longing of the windows,
extends from the tower's body.

Lodged in the starry night, accompanying the dawn,
For the sake of tomorrow's joy,
They use the tower's drumlike arm,
to shoulder the republic's mission tomorrow.

December 5, 1982. Chongqing Mount Gele
(English Trans. Matt Turner and Haiying Weng)

野餐之趣

炊煙裊裊，
鳥兒聲聲，
新鮮，清涼，甜美的氣味，
傳出不同層次的深林。

疲勞的骨骼和窘迫的肺葉，
在深林裡，
在藍天下，
在暖風的嬉戲中，
得到洗新，恢復，休整。

心，
沐浴在嘩嘩的春雨中，
歌，
飄落在墨綠的海洋裡。

1982.4.26於重慶歌樂山下

Picnic Fun

Curls of smoke from cooking fires,

The chirping of birds,

A fresh, cool, sweet fragrance,

emanate from each level of the forest.

Weary bones and exhausted lungs,

In the forest,

Under the blue sky,

In the play of warm wind,

Refresh, restore, and rejuvenate.

Heart,

bathed in the patter of Spring rain,

Song,

floating in the jasper ocean.

April 26, 1982. Chongqing Mount Gele
(English Trans. Matt Turner and Haiying Weng)

給開拓者

我探尋著，
在巍岩的斷紋裡，
探尋出，
一根跳動延伸的神經。

我輕彈著，
在萌動的綠草間，
輕彈出，
一排雲雀搏擊長空的飛鳴。

1982.1 於重慶歌樂山下

For the Pathbreakers

I am seeking,

Amongst the rock's broken lines,

To draw out,

A nerve that beats and expands.

I am flickering,

Between the sprouting green grass,

Flaring up,

A row of skylarks pound the sky with their song.

January 1982. Chongqing Mount Gele

(English Trans. Matt Turner and Haiying Weng)

生活

床，碗，
課堂，水泥路，
拆散，組合成一個四度空間。

四方的床，青瓷的碗，
整潔的教室，淺灰的路，
還有萬花筒似的試管。

我盯著萬花筒的色彩，
旋轉，
矯正的焦距，
窗口，
滾翻著我多彩的生活，
流出我燦爛的和諧。

1981.10 於重慶歌樂山下

Student Life

A bed, a bowl,
classroom, cement road,
disjoin, merge into four dimensions.

A square bed, a celadon bowl,
tidy lecture hall, light grey road,
and the kaleidoscope-like test tubes.

I gaze into the colors of the kaleidoscope,
gyrating,
the adjusted focus,
at the window,
my colorful life rolls over,
overflowing with splendid harmony.

October 1981. Chongqing Mount Gele
(English Trans. Matt Turner and Haiying Weng)

力的旋律
——題同名壁畫

滾翻，
　　　臂的肌腱；
旋轉，
　　　火球的光圈；
在湛藍的天體中，
光的飛進與火輪的呼嘯，
　　　　　　爆炸出，
　　　　力的閃電！

1983.9 於重慶歌樂山下

Melodies of Force
——After a mural of the same title

Roll over,

    The arm's bicep;

Rotate,

    The aperture of the fireball.

In the azure galaxy,

Light bursts forth and the fiery wheel howls,

        Blasting forth,

      The lightning of force!

September 1983. Chongqing Mount Gele
(English Trans. Matt Turner and Haiying Weng)

春之校園

校園，
一片新綠，
林中簇擁著一株株桃紅，
圖書館前印下的一串串腳印，
閱覽室裡藏著的深邃的記憶，
晨露中帶濕的書聲，
濃霧中飛跑的腳步聲。

這是春的資訊，
這是春的細語。

晨散發出它的清新，
新雨洗滌了路上的舊痕，
輕拂曙色的涼風，
送來了春天的鈴聲。

啊！校園的春天，
　　鮮美的校園。

1981.10.1於重慶歌樂山下

Campus in Spring

The campus,

A plot of new green,

Peach-red clustered together in the trees,

Lines of footprints leading from the library,

Profound memories hidden in the reading room,

Damp recitation in the dew,

Footsteps racing in the fog.

This is Spring's message,

This is Spring's whispers.

Morning gives off its freshness,

New rain washes old marks off the road,

The cool breeze kisses the new dawn,

Rings in the bell of Spring.

O! Spring on campus,

Breathtaking campus.

October 1, 1980. Chongqing Mount Gele
(English Trans. Matt Turner and Haiying Weng)

時辰

綠葉，
流汁的蘋果，
在晶瑩的雨點中，
滴下！

成熟，
潑灑的月光，
在突騰的浪尖上，
崛起！

1982.4.25於重慶歌樂山下

Time

Green leaf,
Juicy apple,
In sparkling raindrops,
drips down!

Maturity,
A splash of moonlight,
On the crests of surging waves,
arises!

April 25, 1982. Chongqing Mount Gele
(English Trans. Matt Turner and Haiying Weng)

螢火蟲

黑暗裡，
你是一盞燈，
和繁星一同
分享人間的寧靜。

天亮了，
你擦掉了最後一滴淚，
然後，
熄滅了，
和太陽一起擁抱永恆。

1982.3.20 於重慶歌樂山下

Firefly

In the dark,

You are a lamp,

Along with the stars

share tranquility in the world.

It's daybreak,

You wipe away the last tear,

And then,

Putting it out,

Embracing eternity along with the sun.

March 20, 1983. Chongqing Mount Gele

(English Trans. Matt Turner and Haiying Weng)

陽臺上

黑夜旋轉過河心，
霧散了。

陽臺上，
一盆蝴蝶花招搖，
頭上懸著一輪太陽，
繽彩的光影拂動，
點綴著如夢的花牆。

牽引起一片蔚藍，
窺視隱逸的月亮。

天真的細手抖著彩飛的蝴蝶，
遐思的眼神托起晶瑩的臉龐，
喜悅的心靈溢出在暖暖的掌上，
啊！驚喜的小姑娘。

1982.6.1於重慶歌樂山下

On the Balcony

Night rotates through the river,
The fog scatters.

On the balcony,
A pot of irises flaunts itself,
The sun hangs over its head,
Colorful shadows flicker,
Adorning the dreamlike lattice wall.

Pull up a slice of azure,
To spy on the retreating moon.

Innocent, slim hands shake the colorful butterfly,
Contemplative eyes hold up the beaming face,
The joyous soul running over the warm, open palms,
Oh, A surprising little girl!

June 1, 1982, Chongqing Mount Gele
(English Trans. Matt Turner and Haiying Weng)

別送

你目送著我，
擠進車裡；
全部的思緒，
聚成一粒，
黏在含淚的窗口；
你情著我，
我噙著你。

相撞的焦點，
各自相送；
我乘著白雲走了，
牽退了的你，
仍佇立山頂，
落日的黃昏裡。

1981.9於踏水鄉

Seeing Off

You're following me with your eyes,
Squeezing into the car.
All of your emotions,
Rolled into a single spot,
Stuck on the teary window.
You're immersed into me,
I'm holding you in my eyes.

The focus point where we clash,
Is when we send each other off;
I rode away on a white cloud,
The vanishing you,
Still standing on mountaintop,
In a dusky sunset.

September 1981. Stepping Water Village
(English Trans. Matt Turner and Haiying Weng)

海灘

昨晚，
我徜徉在沙灘金帶邊，
遠遠地，
我望見泛藍的大海上，
　　輕漾著一條小舢，
　　和一片閃銀的帆，
正在尋找她歸航的港灣。

昨晚，
我失落在微波的港灣，
悄悄地，
我發現在朦朧的幽夢裡，
泊著一葉張開的銀帆，
在巡視她出港的航線。

海的澀，
波的鹹，
海鷗的執著，
白雲的信念，
昨晚，我夢見一閃銀帆，
駛出港口，奔向蔚藍。

1982.12 於重慶歌樂山下

The Beach

Last night,
I strolled along a long golden belt,
and far, far out,
I saw the azure ocean,
    A rippling little boat,
    And a flickering silver sail,
Searching for a port for her to return.

Last night,
I lost my way in the bay with gentle waves,
And stealthily, stealthily,
I discovered hidden in a moonlit dream,
An open silver sail moors,
inspecting the route of her departure.

The astringent sea,
The salty waves,
The tenacious seagull,
The conviction of the white cloud,
Last night, when I dreamed of a silver sail flickering,
set out to port, and heading towards the azure.

December 1982. Chongqing Mount Gele
(English Trans. Matt Turner and Haiying Weng)

贈友

──在孩提時，
我的夥伴們拋著弧形的繩索，
我們嬉笑著在繩圈中穿越，
一圈，一圈，又一圈……

當我倘徉在河灘，
在水波裡，我總把我黑色的背影發現；
當我穿行在茂密的樹林，
我總發現一塊蠕動的翳蔭；
當我拂風在斜陽的花間，
我總發現太陽光子中的斑點。

哦！我多麼希望水波逐浪，
把我的背影殉葬；
我多麼希望太陽能直耀，
把我的陰影收藏；
我多麼希望花間孕朝露，
使花露閃爍螢光。

我真希望奔向遠方，
對你，
對我，
我們將永遠不再在
繩圈中「絕唱」。

For a Friend

During my childhood,

My playmates swung an arc rope,

We jumped through the circle with laughter,

One loop, another loop, and another ······

When I walk on the beach,

In the waves, I always catch sight of my black shadow;

When I walk through the dense forest,

I always find a creeping shade;

When I'm brushed by the wind through flowers at sunset,

I always come upon flecks of sunlight.

O! How I want the waves to ripple,

to bury my shadow.

How I wish sun could shine straight through,

to collect my shadow.

How I wish flowers could nurture morning dews,

to make the flower's dews lustrous.

How I want to run far away,

For you,

For me,

Where we will never, ever,

sing the "swan song" in the circles of the rope.

我真希望在這裡，
我真希望在空曠中，
在我們的掌心裡，
永流著希望繁生的力量。

1982.12.25 於踏水鄉

All I really want here,

I really want the wide open,

In the palms of our hands,

To always overflow with the strength of hope.

December 25, 1982. Stepping Water Village
(English Trans. Matt Turner and Haiying Weng)

心思

——贈學友
某君贈我一首不完整的詩，
我有幸抄錄下來以此回贈。

夜，飄著香馨，
破碎的月光漏過真空的防護林，
安撫著一顆憂傷的心，
以及河邊絳紫色的小花，
還有一個映著背影的遊人，
哦！不會欺騙我吧？
我的夢，我的精靈！

火車啟動了，
嘶鳴的鋼軌，砸砸聲聲，
碾碎了遠遊人的心，
從鋼輪軸心噴出的音符，
愈遠，愈深，愈沉，
請相信吧，「我的歌，我的靈」！

這羊腸小徑，延展無際，
彎彎曲曲，宛如江河，
通向大地肺葉的深處，
經千萬年的延伸，聚合，
竟造化出這麼謎一般的叩問，
繼續前行吧，「我的寄託，我的追索」！

1982.7.6 於踏水鄉

Random Thoughts

——For a school friend
Someone gave me an incomplete poem,
I was lucky enough to copy it down as a gift in return.

Night, fragrance wafting,
Broken moonlight leaks through the vacuum of shelter forest,
To soothe a grieving heart,
And the riverbed's purplish little flowers,
And also a wanderer with his reflective shadow,
Oh – you won't cheat me?
My dream, my spirit!

The train has fired up,
The whine of the rails grinds out sound,
Crushing the wanderer's heart,
Notes bursting from steel wheel's axle shaft,
Farther, deeper, darker,
Please believe me: "My song, my soul!"

The winding little trail goes on and on,
Twisting and turning like a river,
Into the recesses of the earth's lungs,
And after thousands of years of unfurling, converge,
Creating such puzzling questions,
Please move on: "My hope, my quest!"

July 6, 1982. Stepping Water Village
(English Trans. Matt Turner and Haiying Weng)

新年小贈

去年，
流溢著輕漾的醉心；
陽光的迴旋，
鳴起跳躍的詩弦，
我吟融了幻夢與清曼的短存。

今年，
奏著一個輕快的小贈，
驚夢的銀剪，唰唰
切飛瞳仁的霧點，
簌簌地我周遭這非凡的人生。

明年，
詠起一葉輕舟的殷勤，
波心的織豔，
色複著滾動的譴綣，
我沉浸在光與清，靈與泉的秘境。

1982.12.31 於踏水鄉

A Little New Year's Gift

Last year,

I was overflowing with the ripples of infatuation.

The revolving of the sunlight,

Sounded out a dancing poem on a string,

 I chanted a transience of the dream and gentle heart.

This year,

I played a cheerful little melody,

A surprising dream like silver scissors, *shua-shua*,

cutting off the mist around the pupil,

I rustled away this abnormal life.

Next year,

I'll chant the graciousness of a leaf-like boat,

The charm in the heart of the wave,

reverberates the rolling attraction,

I'm immersed in the mystic world of light and clarity, soul and spring.

December 31, 1982. Stepping Water Village
(English Trans. Matt Turner and Haiying Weng)

月

一輪鵝黃，鵝黃的新月升起來了，
我駕著一條淺藍的小船出航了。

晶瑩的月鏡，
吸入倩柔的一瞥，
竊走了我饑渴的心，
一首無形的歌在水波中沉浸。

無數條銀練似的光，
輕撫著濕潤的船舷，
搖櫓劃亂了諧和的光波，
一個沉睡的夢漸漸復活。

一輪銀灰，銀灰的月色暗了下去，
我駕著我的小舟也隨波而漂逝。

1982.8.15 於踏水鄉

Moon

A light, light yellow moon came up,
I set sail on a light blue boat.

Glistening moon-mirror,
inhales a soft glance,
It has stolen my hungry heart,
an invisible song sunk in a ripple.

Countless silvery lights,
are stroking the wet boat's sides,
oars disrupt the harmonious waves of light,
a sleepy dream slowly revives.

An ash-, ash-silver moonlight stealthily went down,
And I steered my boat to follow the drift of the waves.

August 15, 1982. Stepping Water Village
(English Trans. Matt Turner and Haiying Weng)

沙的啟示

長江的細浪，
輕拍著橙黃的沙灘，
層層細浪淤積成一塊無邊的梯田，
推移著一個勤勞，憨厚，聰睿的年輪，
沖迭成一副千溝萬壑的沙臉。

這臉面，
帶著痛楚，也顯示悠閒，
是豪放，但也穩健，
伴著滔滔江水，
寧靜地躺在這碧藍，碧藍的
浪花簇擁的岸邊。

這充滿著血和肉的沙灘啊，
濃濃的眉棱，
緊抿的嘴唇？

1982.6.17 於長江沙灘

Sand's Illumination

The Yangtze's gentle waves,
lap the orange beaches,
The waves deposit silt into an endless terrace,
Rolling through a hardworking, honest, and wise growth-ring,
Flushing into thousands of ditches, onto a face of sand.

This face,
It's in pain, yet reveals composure,
It's bold, yet also steadfast.
Along with the surging Yangtze water,
It reclines on the shore,
Encroached upon by the azure waves.

This beach overflows with blood and flesh,
Bushy eyebrows,
Pursed lips?

June 17, 1982. On the Yangtze River Beach
(English Trans. Matt Turner and Haiying Weng)

晨露

當暗夜悄然離去，
黎明輕盈地降臨，
在小徑旁的草尖上，
你正聆聽草間的耳語，
而未聽見黎明的足音。

你是那麼甜蜜，柔順，
那麼亮麗，晶瑩，
你是黑暗的見證，
你是時間的音韻。

我深知你心中的願望，
就是與小草永久依偎，
不害怕太陽光的照耀，
更不埋怨自己的宿命，
你寧可浸入大地的懷抱，
伴著黑土，滋潤全生靈。

1981.3 於踏水鄉

Morning Dew

When night slips away,
Dawn swiftly arrives,
On the tips of the grass by the roadside,
You are listening to the grass whisper,
But not hearing dawn's footsteps.

You are so sweet and gentle,
So shiny, glistening,
You are testimony to darkness,
You are the sound of time.

I know well your heart's desire,
To perpetually lean against the grass,
Not afraid of the light of the sun,
Not complaining about your fate,
You would rather be embraced by the earth,
Along with the black soil, moistening all the creatures.

March 1981. Stepping Water Village
(English Trans. Matt Turner and Haiying Weng)

夕陽

一輪亮光突然收斂成
西邊的一位歸隱；
夕暉慷贈給大地
最後的戀影，
牽浮著萬物的沉淪；
啊！多彩的夕陽，
寶貴的生命！

點點星光的啟迪，
蒼穹的延伸，
西邊的餘暉裡，
流出大寫的我們。

1981. 12 於踏水鄉

Sunset

Light suddenly converges
into a recluse in the west;
Gloaming bestows upon the earth
its last shadow of love,
Draws the fate of all things.
O colorful sunset,
Precious life!

Illuminating starlight,
Sky's extension,
In the afterglow of the west,
overflow us in capital letters.

December 1981. Stepping Water Village
(English Trans. Matt Turner and Haiying Weng)

贈友
——致一位殘廢青年

輪椅滾動著殘缺的完整，
完整的神經支撐起輪椅的生命。

朋友，請站起來吧！
生命不應這樣折騰，
希望不應這樣枯竭，
湛藍的天空大雁飛鳴。

誰說人都是完整，
誰說人生皆一帆風順，
誰說殘缺就失去了創造與青春，
可是我卻要大聲宣告：
「殘缺正激勵每個人去攀登」！

殘缺裡有亮錚錚的骨脊，
殘缺裡有眺望的火熱，
殘缺裡有百折不回的剛毅，
有一種沉默的希望，
有一爆驕傲的新生。

For a Friend
——To a disabled young man

The wheelchair rolls with incomplete integrity
The complete spirit upholds the life of the wheelchair

Friend, please stand up.
Life shouldn't be restless like this,
Hope shouldn't be so exhausted,
In the azure sky the geese soars up.

Who says people are complete,
Who says that life is smooth,
Who says disability means the loss of creation and youth,
But I have to shout out:
Disability encourages everyone to climb higher.

The incompletes have ridges in their bones,
The incompletes have visionary fire,
The incompletes are steadfast in fortitude,
There is silent hope,
There is bursting with new life.

春風輕拂著渴波的垂柳，
秋陽流淌著田野裡的金黃；
桂冠佳壤盼著你去耕耘，
朋友啊！起身吧！
我願青春的熱血在你雙臂上飛騰！

　　　　　　　　　　　　1982.3.4 於岳池縣

The spring breeze blows the desiring willows,

The autumn sun flows across the golden field,

The rich soil anticipates your cultivation,

So friend, rise up.

May the hot blood of youth take you higher.

March 4, 1982. Yuechi County

(English Trans. Matt Turner and Haiying Weng)

勞動之歌

我用汗水澆灌鮮新的田野，
我用鋤頭掘出春天的芳馨，
我用鐮刀收割秋天的金黃，
我用犁鏵耕耘晨露的晶瑩。

我只知道農民對土地的深情，
我只知道勤勞才能翻卷麥浪，
我只知道耕耘層層油黑沃土，
我只知道開墾深邃的大荒涼。

清新，泥土播散的涓涓甘甜，
律動，小河抒發的圈圈波瀾。

我帶著饑渴的綠色希翼，
我披星耕種濕潤的土地，
我堅信日日夜夜的耕耘，
明年秋日那喜悅的收成。

　　　　　　　　　1981.11.18 於重慶歌樂山下

Song of Work

I use sweat to irrigate the fresh fields,
I use a hoe to till Spring's fragrance,
I use a scythe to reap Autumn's gold,
I use a plough to till morning dew's glistening.

I only know the farmer's deep love of the land,
I only know diligence turns the waves of wheat,
I only know ploughing the rich, black soil,
I only know cultivating the deep wilderness.

Fresh, trickling sweetness emanated from the soil,
Rhythm, circling ripples animated from the river.

I'm carrying my hungry green hope,
I plough the wet soil underneath the stars,
I have the conviction in the till of day and night,
A joyful harvest will be reaped next autumn.

November 18, 1981. Chongqing Mount Gele
(English Trans. Matt Turner and Haiying Weng)

小徑

循著這曲折的小路，
邁向大地肺葉的深處，
這曲折蜿蜒的小徑啊，
曾多次焊接，聚合，分裂。

它不止一次鼓動那顫動的肺葉，
檢索著大地以及人類的命運。

終於這條無限延伸的小徑，
凸現一個特大的問號？

我們該走向何處？
這是問號的上耳。

我們該怎樣走向何處？
這是問號烏黑的大底。

1982.2.20 於重慶歌樂山下

Little Trail

Following this circuitous path,
To the depths of the earth's lungs,
O this circuitous, serpentine path,
It has joined many times, converging and dividing.

More than once it tickled the trembling lungs,
Inspected the fate of mankind and the earth.

Finally, this endlessly extending trail,
It comes to a great question mark.

Where should we go?
It's the question mark's ear.

How should we get there?
It's the question mark's big black butt.

February 20, 1982. Chongqing Mount Gele
(English Trans. Matt Turner and Haiying Weng)

零點

天空突然同時分娩，
一半飄然離去，
一半輕盈跨前，
這相交的時辰就是：零點！

在零點，
我們正駕著新月的幽夢，
我們正乘著翔羽的涼風，
從赤壁的廢墟進發，
開到鏖戰的最前沿。

去揭開歷史的扉頁，
去搏擊洪峰的浪尖，
瞭望新理想的繽彩，
零點，我正屏著呼吸，
跟隨繁星滑動的方向。

1982.1.1 於踏水鄉

Midnight

Suddenly, at the same time, the sky gave birth,

Half drifting away,

Half striding lightly ahead,

The time of their meeting: the zero hour!

At the zero hour,

We're riding the new moon's mystic dream,

We're riding the wings of the cool breeze,

Starting out from the ruins of Red Cliff,

We advance to the front lines of battle.

To leaf open history's title page,

To fight against the flood tide,

Gazing into the colors of the new ideals,

At the zero hour, I hold my breath,

and follow the guide of the gliding stars.

January 1, 1982. Stepping Water Village

(English Trans. Matt Turner and Haiying Weng)

燕語

你是春天的信使，
你輕輕的呢喃，
婉轉的歌喉，
點破河水的清波，
喚來旖旎的春光。

你是季候的忠實聽者，
嘴裡綻開花朵，
從飄香的南國，
跋涉千山萬水，
飛到雪簇的北疆，
劃出天空下的春色。

你揮動著銀色的雙翼，
穿行於暖風拂柳之間，
這裡已是初春的氣息。

啊！當你滿載喜顏，
飛過我的田園，
你可知道，那兒早已
繁花盛開，百鳥喧天。

1981.3 於踏水鄉

The Chirping of Swallows

You are the messenger of Spring,

Your soft whisper,

and mild singing,

Ripple the river's clear waves,

Calling out Spring's charming scenery.

You are the season's loyal listener,

Flowers bursting from the mouth,

From the fragrant south,

Across many mountains and rivers,

To the snowy, northern border,

Drawing Spring out under the sky.

You flap your silver wings,

across the warm wind and the willows,

Here comes the smell of early Spring.

O, when you are full of joy,

Flying over my fields,

May you know, it's already there

A world of blooming flowers and singing birds.

March 1981, Stepping Water Village
(English Trans. Matt Turner and Haiying Weng)

校園的音波

是微風發出輕柔的呼喚？
是河水攪碎了的藍天？
啊！沉默多年的魔音，
終於通過揚聲器的弧圈，
傳遍了春意的校園。

一串串悅耳的音符，
傳遞著春光的資訊，
乳燕的翩翩呢喃，
這音符在教室，在食堂，
在辦公室，在幼稚園，
輕盈地躍動，迴旋。

清晨，每當我們從夢中驚醒，
我們那水晶般的腦海裡，
便住滿了激勵的音樂，詩歌，
不，首先傳到我耳膜的是
我們日日曆練的生活。

啊！是的，我們煉獄般的跋涉，
實在需要彩旗來飄蕩，鼓動，
通過電波的暗壁，在距離的空間，
沁出迷醉的旋律，那是美的讚歌。

1981.12.13 於重慶歌樂山下

The Sounds of Campus

Is the breeze softly calling?
Has the river broken the azure sky?
O demonic sound, after years of silence,
Finally, through the loudspeaker's coil,
The sound spreads across Spring's campus.

A sequence of pleasant notes,
passing Spring's message on,
The whispering of the young swallows,
The notes in the classroom, in the canteen,
In the office, in the kindergarten,
are lightly leaping, and swirling.

Every morning, when we are jolted from dreams,
Our crystal minds
Are full of inspiring music and poetry,
But no, the first thing to reach my eardrum
is the daily life we are living through.

O yes, our trek through purgatory,
really calls for colored banners that flutter and inspire,
Through the dark radio waves, far in the distance,
Exuding an intoxicating melody, a hymn to beauty.

December 13, 1981. Chongqing at Mount Gele
(English Trans. Matt Turner and Haiying Weng)

小息

竹林
青青
江水
靜靜
一葉扁舟伴溪岸
試問主人在何方？
請看竹林深處
煙火映紅的臉
那安坐船頭
叼著煙袋的老漁民

1981.4.5 於嘉陵江邊

A Little Rest

Bamboo grove

Light green

River's water

Still, calm

Skiff in the stream bed

Where is the owner?

Look into the depths of the grove

Fire from smoke flushes the face

Sitting quietly at the prow

An old fisherman with his pipe in his mouth

April 5, 1981. At Jialing River bank
(English Trans. Matt Turner and Haiying Weng)

我愛雪花

我愛雪花，
我愛被雪花點綴的世界，
雖然我在南方長大，
但這愛已從小就在心中萌芽。

在童夢裡媽媽就告訴我，
「你要愛就愛雪花吧！」
幼時並不懂這句話的含義，
只知道雪花是白色的「花。」

我愛雪花，
從我挎上書包那天起，
到走過十八春秋的歲月，
我心中一直惦著媽媽的話。

我愛每一朵飄柔的雪花，
山邊冬梅散發出的雪香，
漂浮在江河上面的雪冰，
收割後稻田裡的雪霜。

我愛雪花，
人間萬物經她的洗禮，
變得更加聖潔無暇，
她寧願自己消失，
也要換來春天的鳥語花香。

1981.4.15 於踏水鄉

I Love Snowflakes

I love snowflakes,
I love a world dotted with snowflakes,
Although I grew up in the south,
The love sprouted in my heart at a young age.

In a child's dream my mother told me,
"If you want to love, love snowflakes!"
At the time I didn't understand what she meant,
Only that snowflakes were "flakey."

I love snowflakes,
From that day I strapped on my book bag,
Through 18 years of Spring and Autumn,
I've always thought about my mother's words.

I love every single floating flake of snow,
The fragrance of snow by the winter plum on the hill,
Slush floating on the river,
Frost after harvesting the rice paddies.

I love snowflakes,
All things are baptized by her,
and become holy and pure,
She would rather disappear,
As an exchange with blossoming Spring.

April 15, 1981. Stepping Water Village
(English Trans. Matt Turner and Haiying Weng)

情的暖流
——題同名壁畫

從一片朦朧的星雲的漏縫中，
流動著太陽光茫萬丈的喜悅，
月亮暢飲後的酣睡，
傳來了風的催促，
飄來了霧的消亡，
揀起一縷筆直的通亮，
揉成一條旋動的光圈，
纏在手指上飛舞翩翩。

這通光亮，
有自己的光源，
有自己的流向，
在繽紛彩舞中，
噴射出無限光芒。

　　　　　　　　　　1982.5.3 於重慶歌樂山下

Current of Emotion
——After a mural of the same title

From a crack in the misty nebula,

The lofty joy of sunlight flows out,

The sleep of moonlight after a drink.

Wind has rushed in,

And the fog has dissipated,

Picking up a ray of light,

Kneading it into a spinning halo,

Tangled on the fingers, prancing.

This ray of light,

With its own source of light,

With its own direction,

In a colorful dance,

bursts forth infinite radiance.

May 3, 1982. Chongqing Mount Gele
(English Trans. Matt Turner and Haiying Weng)

湖濱雪韻

水融化了雪花的潔淨，
湖底蘊藏著春的暖情，
我歡望著小橋，
小路卻引導了我的目光，
墜落在空寂的涼亭，
冰涼的心，
寄託在清冷的涼亭，
愛的涼亭，
波的真誠。

1981.3.28 於踏水鄉

Snow Rhythm of the Lakeside

The water thaws the snow's cleanliness,

The lakebed hides the warmth of Spring,

I'm gazing at the little bridge,

But the little path guides my eyes,

descending to the empty pavilion,

Frozen heart,

Left on the desolate pavilion,

The pavilion of love,

The sincerity of ripples.

March 28, 1981. Stepping Water Village
(English Trans. Matt Turner and Haiying Weng)

思憶

1.

我思憶，
孩子的遊戲，
思緒的飛奔，
響箭一樣快，
雪一樣白。

高高的山頂上，
霞光撒滿
幽深的深林，
細草扎根在山頂。

突然，我鑽進了
赤裸的密林。

Remembrances

1.

I remember,
Children's games,
Thoughts flying ahead,
As fast as arrows,
As white as snow.

High, high on the hilltop
Rays of light everywhere,
A deep forest,
Grass rooted into the hilltop.

Then suddenly, I found myself
In the midst of a naked, dense wood.

2.

思緒，
彷徨中的憧憬，
像久旱後的甘霖，
像斷弦的弓音，
明澄的天空下，
麋鹿飛越闌珊。

朦朧中，雙手舉頭，
摘下一片彩雲。

1981.8.20 於踏水鄉

2.

Thoughts,

The longing in hesitation,

Like the downpour after the drought,

Like the sound of a snapped string,

Under the clear sky,

The elks cross over the fence.

In the mist, raising both hands above my head,

I pick out a colorful cloud.

August 20, 1981. Stepping Water Village
(English Trans. Matt Turner and Haiying Weng)

致老師

您用通亮的白色光體，
在這個聳立的四方形空間，
劃出條條啟蒙的軌跡，
勾繪著青春閃爍的宏願。

如果說這四方形裡縱橫的線條，
就像蜘蛛網上神祕的糾纏，
那您就高舉閃亮的火炬，
燃亮蜘蛛網上那致命的黑洞，
揭開通往真理的大道。

那火炬也照亮您的鬢霜，
和那網狀的層層皺紋。

1981.9.9 於重慶歌樂山下

To the Teacher

You used a bright white light,
In this huge square space,
To lay out the path to enlightenment,
Outlining the aspirations of youth.

If the vertical and horizontal lines of this square space,
are like the mystery of a spider web,
Then you hold a shining torch up high,
Burning a fatal black hole into the web,
Revealing the great way to truth.

The torch also illuminates your white hair,
and layer upon layer of your furrows.

September 9, 1981. Chongqing Mount Gele
(English Trans. Matt Turner and Haiying Weng)

公共汽車駕駛員之歌

路燈，眨著惺忪的睡眼，
涼風，刮過黎明前的街道，
「笛笛、笛笛」清脆竄起，
打破了寧靜的夜色，
鑽進人們熟睡的窗櫺。

你們載著早行的旅客，
從條條街上穿過，
辛勤的你們，精神振奮，
開始一天的往返奔波。

你們熟練地把握方向盤，
轉彎抹角，上坡下坎，
雙眼始終閃著機靈的光芒，
熾熱的脈搏點亮黎明的燈火，
莊嚴的大地期待你們的穿梭。

有人非難你們工作枯燥無味，
你們卻奏出「笛笛」的弦音，
展示你們心中的快樂；
有人蔑視你的工作平凡無功，
你們卻把高傲的頭顱一轉，
齊聲呼喊車裡滿載的夥伴。

A Song for Bus Drivers

Streetlights blinking their sleepy eyes,
Cool wind scraping the street before dawn,
Honk-honk, honk-honk, clear and crisp,
Cracking through the still night,
Drilling into the windows of people's sleep.

You carry the morning travelers,
From street to street,
Your hard work, high spirit,
Begin your back-and-forth for the day.

Your masterly command of the steering wheel,
Twisting and turning, up and down hills,
Eyes flashing with a clever spirit,
A blazing pulse lighting the dawn,
The solemn earth looks forward to your shuttling.

Some people reproach your job as boring,
But you play out a honking tune,
Showing the joy in your heart;
Some people look down on your job as mundane,
But you turn your proud head,
And call to the friends loaded on the bus.

啊！你們車前的反光鏡，
映照出你們潔白的心靈，
無私奉獻的真誠，
「平凡的工作，崇高的信仰！」
你們駕駛著勞動的喜悅，
馳進原野，跨過山崗，
去迎接射入人間的第一縷光束，
一個璀璨而又清新的黎明。

　　　　　　　　　　　1982.6.20 於重慶歌樂山下

O your rearview mirror,

reflects your pure spirit,

Selfless devotion,

"Ordinary work, lofty belief!"

You are driving the joy of labor,

into plains and across hills,

To meet the first beam of light entering the world,

A fresh, bright dawn.

June 20, 1982. Chongqing Mount Gele
(English Trans. Matt Turner and Haiying Weng)

根

風
夾著暴雨
樹
瘋狂搖擺
在這狂風暴雨的撕裂中
樹幹屹然傲立
其實屹立不是樹的軀幹
而是它紮入大地的根

　　　　　　　　　　　　1982.4.6 於重慶歌樂山下

Roots

Wind

Coming in torrents

Tree

Shaking violently

In this rip of a furious storm

The bare trunk stands proudly

Actually that which stands is not the trunk

But the roots which have lodged into the earth

April 6, 1982. Chongqing Mount Gele
(English Trans. Matt Turner and Haiying Weng)

春夏之交

我站在春夏之交的緯線上，

向春看，
桃花謝了，
隨著春；
李花也謝了，
留下滿枝的嫩掛。

向夏看，
沒有花，
但有果，
沒有芳香，
但有火熱，
有日日升起的驕陽。

1982.6.21 於重慶歌樂山下

From Spring to Summer

I stand on a latitude line,

when Spring turns to Summer.

Look to Spring,

Peach blossoms wither,

Following Spring.

Plum blossoms also wither,

Leaving tender sprouts on branches.

Look to Summer,

No flowers,

But there is fruit.

No fragrance,

But there is heat,

And the blazing sun rises each day.

June 21, 1982. Chongqing Mount Gele
(English Trans. Matt Turner and Haiying Weng)

致新同學

新的夥伴，你們來了，
來到了這充滿遐想的海洋。

這裡有清幽的歌樂山巒的流雲，
這裡有秀麗的嘉陵江畔的紅霞，
這裡有六月炙烤的驕陽，
這裡有四月盛開的繁花。

啊！新的夥伴，歡迎你們，
恰在燦爛歡欣的時刻。

你們趟過果林點點的星光，
擷下秋天成熟的每一粒金黃，
採集了秋映楓葉的每一片光華，
攢著秋日田野的每一縷希望。

你們來了，我們歡迎你們呀！
你們帶著母親的重托，
你們帶著長輩的教誨。

豐收的田野需要重新辛勤的耕耘，
勞作的汗水才能換來明秋的佳景，
在這沒有答案的人生征途中哦，
我們衷心祝願你們，祝願你們
吹響進軍的號角，祝願你們

To My New Classmates

New companions, here you come,
Come to this ocean of reverie.

There are Mt Gele's calm clouds,
There is the Jialing River's beautiful sunset,
There is June's scorching sun,
There are April's full blooms.

O new partners, I welcome you,
At this very moment of splendor.

You passed through the stars in the fruit trees,
Pinched off every golden grain that came forth in Autumn,
Collected light from Autumn's maple,
Grasping every last wisp of hope from Autumn's fields.

You have come, and we say welcome!
You have carried your mother's trust,
You have carried your family's teachings.

The abundant field needs to be plowed afresh,
The sweat of your brow will transform next year's Autumn,
O in the middle of this journey full of questions,
We wish you all the best, wish that you
Blow "Revelry" to advance, wish that you

撥動智慧的弦音，祝願你們
毫無畏懼地去攀登，最後祝願你們
明朝的田野鮮花盛開，碩果纍纍。

1982.9.10 於重慶歌樂山下

Pluck the strings of wisdom, wish that you

Are undaunted by the ascent, in the end wish that

The flowers of the future will bloom, full of countless fruits.

September 10, 1982.Chongqing Mount Gele
(English Trans. Matt Turner and Haiying Weng)

雪的白描

多麼誘人的圖畫，
我禁不住走了進去，
雙手捋著雪的素雅，
「吱吱，雪」。

攝影機的鏡頭，
我瞄準視線，
「咔」溶化我與雪的交影，
「吱吱，雪」。

手揉著一梅花瓣，
碎了，碎了，
碎瓣黏住了我砰跳的心，
「吱吱，雪」。

赤腳惦著這清淨的柔，
雙眼噙著這柔柔的細，
我應約而至，
「吱吱，雪」。

A Light Sketch of Snow

Such an attractive picture,
I can't help but walking in,
Both hands brushing the elegance of snow,
"Squeak, squeak – snow."

I focus it,
The camera's lens ,
The click dissolves my shadow in snow,
"Squeak, squeak – snow."

Hand rubbing a plum petal,
Breaking it, breaking it,
Broken petals stuck all over my pumping heart,
"Squeak, squeak – snow."

Barefoot, thinking about this clean softness,
The soft, the fine, all held in my eyes,
I arrive for our appointment,
"Squeak, squeak – snow."

我來尋雪的純真，
我來吮雪的清新，
我來心存雪的潔，
「吱吱，雪」。

1982.12.25 於重慶歌樂山下

I've come to find snow's innocence,

I've come to suckle snow's freshness,

I've come to keep snow's purity,

"Squeak, squeak – snow."

December 25, 1982, Chongqing Mount Gele
(English Trans. Matt Turner and Haiying Weng)

晚歸的老人

鋤頭扛在肩上，
晚歸的腳步行在田埂，
夕陽的餘暉映照眉棱，
一隻紅蜻蜓飛上桑椹。

啊！老人收工的好心情，
連著黏在腳上新鮮的黃泥，
倒映在晚風吹拂的那一片
金燦燦的稻田裡，嵌進
那壕溝深深的皺紋間。

老人的腳步聲剛傳到家門口，
立即跑來可愛的小黃狗，
舔舔老人的腳跟以及那
經筋爆綻的雙手，
老人彎下了腰，
手扶狗頭，喚喚聲聲，
然後面面依偎似知心好友。

1981.8.20 於踏水鄉

The Old Man Who Returned Home Late

Hoe resting on shoulder,
Late-returning footsteps on the ridge,
The setting sun casts its glow across the brow,
Red dragonfly flies onto a mulberry.

O! In a good mood the old man calls it a day,
Fresh yellow mud sticking to his feet,
They are reflected in the evening wind
And in the golden rice paddies, embedded
Between furrows deep as gullies.

The old man's footsteps have just passed the doorway,
And a cute little yellow dog pounces out,
Licking the old man's heels as well as
The veiny hands,
The old man bends down,
pats the dog's head, greets him,
Like old friends nuzzling together.

August 20, 1981. Stepping Water Village
(English Trans. Matt Turner and Haiying Weng)

印刷工人之歌

轟鳴的軋機聲，
在敲動著智慧的暗門，
烏黑的鉛字翻滾，
溢出沁人心扉的光明，
揭開知識神祕的封印。

十指揀字如紡錘，
織出秀麗的錦緞，
使冰冷的鉛字溫暖，
賦予飽滿的體溫與生命，
開啟文明進步的窗櫺。

每當我手握新書，
我就聞到油墨的清香，
而每一個方塊字就是
你們額上油滑的汗粒，
每一頁翻起便是你們
生命不可擦去的深深軌跡。

1983.5.20 於重慶歌樂山下

The Printer's Song

The growl of the grinding mill,
knocking on the dim door of wisdom,
The jet-black type turns over,
overflowing, permeating light,
unveiling the mysteries of knowledge.

The ten fingers arrange the type like a spindle,
weaving beautiful brocade,
warming the cold typeface,
giving off heat and life,
opening the window to civilization.

Every time I hold a new book,
I smell the fresh scent of ink,
and every square word is
a bead of slick sweat on your forehead,
and every turn of the page is your
deep trajectory which cannot be erased by fate.

May 20, 1983. Chongqing Mount Gele
(English Trans. Matt Turner and Haiying Weng)

母校之歌

您從秀麗的嘉陵江畔，
載著長江滔滔的浪花，
經過北碚的曲折風險，
來到巍巍的歌樂山巒。

您經受住了寒風的橫掃，
也頂住了驕陽的炙烤，
從重重濃霧的圍繞中，
掙脫了沉重的枷鎖與腳鐐。

您帶著您的好兒女，
這些共和國明天的生命，
融入色澤魅麗，深邃碧藍，
充滿了生機勃發的海洋裡，
為發現，創新，而暢遊，尋覓。

1982.5.24 於重慶歌樂山下

A Song for My Alma Mater

You come from the beautiful Jialing River,

Carrying the Yangtze's surging waves,

Across Chongqing's rifts and hazards,

You come to towering Mount Gele.

You've weathered cold winds,

Withstood grilling under the roasting sun,

From within a layered and dense fog,

You broke free from heavy shackles and fetters.

You've taken your children,

The lives of tomorrow's nation,

blended into the living, thriving sea,

A colorful, deep blue-green sea,

to explore, to search, for discovery, for innovation.

May 24, 1982. Chongqing Mount Gele
(English Trans. Matt Turner and Haiying Weng)

仿沁園春

春光融融，綿綿細雨，綠柳瀟灑。
聽滿園燕語，蜂飛蝶舞，蓓蕾初綻，
一片生機。

青竹節節，泉水潺潺，群山碧水春意繞。
凝神聽，種子萌破土，春光普照。
望西邊掛彩霞，篝火燃燒，幻麗星空鳥兒香夢早。

晨露浸桃花，鮮潤豐澤，韶華橫飄，揮戈正好。
巡視大地，潔淨輕紗，改革開放祖國換新貌。

展明朝，春雷陣陣，祖國富饒。

1981.4.21於踏水鄉

In Imitation of *Qinyuan Chun*

Joyous spring light, continuous drizzle, elegant green willow.
Listen to the swallows talk, bees and butterflies dance, the buds bloom,
Full of signs of life in the garden.

Steady bamboo, bubbling springs, Spring seeps into the mountains
and the water.
Listen carefully, to seeds sprouting from the earth, to the Spring light
illuminating all.
See the rosy clouds in the west, the bonfire burning, the dreams of
birds in the starry sky.

Peach blossom's steeped in morning dew, fresh and exuberant, the
glories of youth marching forward.
Patrolling the earth, cleaning the veil, reform and openness renew the
face of the nation.

Looking ahead to the future, Spring thunders, and the nation is prosperous.

April 4, 1981. Stepping Water Village
(English Trans. Matt Turner and Haiying Weng)

歌樂囈語：詩歌隨筆

　　父親算命問卦，歸，秘籤拆開，字諭：「犬吠密雲，大吉！」母
親振作精神，神祕地將我降生在這個世界。我屬兔，膽小怕駭。

　　小時候，母親珍惜詞彙，菜桑葉貼我的肚臍，防風濕；拿麻紙蓋
我的天靈蓋，避太陽，這樣風風雨雨許多年，我被灌注讚賞而高傲的
形容詞，因此我喜愛典故和成語。

　　獨上高樓的一天引發了我對遠方理想世界的嚮往，從此便開始填
詞寫詩，替古人流淚，學著表達機巧與偶合，感發真實與具體，以詞
彙預卜未來的河流。幾千個日子撲騰而去，一隻大鳥始終繞著我，日
子被一種影子覆蓋，我時時倍感憂慮，隱約總有一天我會被顛覆，成
為理想的獵物。而日復一日的意外事件加重了季節，也不斷攪動我不
安的心靈。為了完善性格，我擁抱時間之流，力圖實踐一種習慣，一
種體認生存與理想的回環狀態。生活在新建設時代的詩人們都應盡力
去理解人民的良心和他們往返的步劃。

　　每當我著手構思一首詩時，我首先想到詩一種超驗的神祕語言，
然後才賦予它們以具體而真實的事件和欲念。詩興襲來之時，我隨即
閉目內視詩歌發生的生動場景，氛圍，盡量在動筆之前測繪繆斯降臨
的路徑，以便在表達時讓詩行自主運行，油然而生，我的心思被詩歌
的不期而遇席捲而走，我並沒有在寫詩，而是詩在寫我，所以請別問
我每首詩的含義，我早已放棄了詩歌的解釋權。詩神啊，請溫柔地用
你的魔笛去開啟讀者迷惑的心靈吧。

　　我始終被生活在我周圍朝夕相處的人民的熱情和耐心所觸動，
他們的生活實在，具體，他們每時每刻都在用詞彙傳達彼此心底最善
良，最勇敢的願望和體諒，而正是這種現實的願望和體諒激發了我憂
鬱的同情心，加深了我最基本的理解力，使我不想掙脫，也無法掙
脫。我必須以一種精力和責任感建造一個理想而新奇的王國，使他們

由每天具體的工作而帶來的焦灼的疲憊和惰性得以自然舒緩；使他們的生存狀態不至於淡漠成娛樂性快感的重複和有機心理意識的淺薄。

****

　　詩是一種生命，如死亡，不可替換。

　　詩的宣泄是一種夢中失眠，一種亢奮的自足，因此詩可以治病，可以返老還童，延年益壽。

　　詩應該建構一種結構衝動。你念完一首詩，就像念動一棵樹，全身劇烈顫抖，熾熱如樹上的火焰突入你的血液，細胞和精脈。你的所有觸識融化為一種醉意，一縷升騰的雲煙。你頓覺自己在打開一扇扇門，而又被一扇扇門反閉。你被擠壓在一團透明的中心：標向丟失，你只得屏息怒放的意念，擇路突圍，而你的呼吸和撫摸卻永遠遺忘在身後的花園，成為遺址和姓氏，你仰天慶賀，你閉目念叨並拾柳葉占卜歸山的日子。

　　To be or not to be。最高級的詩亦是最簡單的詩。拾級而上的努力，雨中俯身揀傘的姿勢，也可以寫成最動人的詩行。「朴」，複歸於嬰兒。雪中的貓和爐火旁的手套也能感動天下所有的良人如泣如訴。

　　詩介入生活如「折若木以拂日」，是一種痛苦理想。「蒼山如海，殘陽如血，」詩人應對客體事件作遠觀的把握，在遠觀中展示憂患刻骨的滲視，建造一種親切的神祕感。詩人在作品中須分裂自己的全部感官，成為無數個陌生人，以創造節奏和氛圍的跌宕和變異。如果揮霍生命，被剝光靈肉，以赤條條的軀體，我們怎能回答懸崖上死者的逼視和囑託呢？以巨大的冷靜招呼我們的人民高尚起來，這就是我們的最大的耐心。

　　詩人是軟體的劊子手，衣冠楚楚，文質彬彬，年輕的和年老的都拄著雕花拐杖，掠奪亡靈們口袋裡的隱私，但關節炎一旦發作他們便溫柔地舉起拐杖，向你——生者，開炮。三藩市一對戀人絕命於金門大橋。

　　詩是對生命之流和人類源極最本真的體驗。我們擦試第一次偶然的血跡時所顯示的率真的惶恐，我們第一次洗去新衣服上的污點而從此養成了愛清潔的習慣。這意味著什麼呢？我們的血液裡至今還流著先祖們高昂的夯歌和玄秘的伐木聲，我們為什麼不熱愛詩歌呢？我的人民，我的同胞？

　　詩是一種情感智化的純粹的複合體，它並不向人們昭示詩人個人隱私的意圖和契機，它是一種蠕動的氛圍，一團布滿了窗眼的空氣，能暢入暢出。在剎那的翻掌間，能使人隨即嗅到詩行中轉機的氣息。詩是一種大腦熱燒後的靜態意識，一種記憶再造的形構，它源於靜默中升起的無弦音樂，並在詞語的誘導下，實現人類直悟智慧的釋放和詩人冥想事件感的升華。

　　寫詩是一種心境，一種語感，它在娓娓的敘述中潛伏詩人的意念和體味，我深信它並不企求任何功利的及時行樂或廉價的憐憫。

　　詩的品質體不在於詞的強度（虛飾性），亦不在於空間感的強度（虛幻性），而在於心境意識的強度（張力性）。詩人對自然，人生的直接領悟應棄絕知識的重疊，而應訴諸心境的整體契合（心緒，心情，心悟，心淨）。在無騷亂的靜息中，詩人便完成了對事件本身的溶解和表達。

　　一首詩應流動一個完整的內在節奏，哪怕是最現代的詩作亦應如此。詩行的弦律應分化在心緒的整合所造成的基調轉突展示中。

　　詩人應具有很強的自控力，過分的躁動不安只能導致他們染上愛混亂的壞習慣，損壞他們最富有能量的運思的自然發揮。而讀詩的人應富有耐心和虔誠感，在在這樣一個忙於誇誇其談的年代裡，連一首高級的詩也值不了幾個硬幣。所以，我一直對這一點深信不疑。男性太注重溫情，女性太看重功利。對當今的讀者來說，他們多數為了尋求愛情或追憶愛情，把詩當作一個更衣室，匆匆忙忙，著上麗裝，婚宴便開始了。哎，走馬觀花的時節真令人心碎。

　史詩已成為神話，對史詩的任何攀登終將是一場企望。訊潮在心中湧動，我走在人類最後一塊棲息地的黃金道上，在我止足之際，我聽見了身後豹子躡足花園的聲音，恢弘而親切。

　詩源生於一個神祕的的非在之地，一種烏托邦式的敞開，一次頌揚生命祕密的挽歌，一股創生宇宙並使之延續，凝融的活力及生機感，它以頌歌的形式得以傳揚。詩悲悼死亡並通過哀悼使生命得以再生。詩所捕捉的失落與死亡並非某些倍感傷痛而難以刻骨銘心的創傷，而是某種並未失落，消滅的東西，詩心始終纏繞於現在及生者，在記憶中召魂，呼喚，啟動起死之大禮，並使過去在記憶的追思緬懷中終於學會了教誨生者，教導現在，亦即，學會了去生活並創造更美好的生活，學會了為未來的生命而生活，一種死後而再生的倖存，一種經由精靈般的蹤跡和生命的餘存點悟和模塑的生命本真。

　難得生存，也難得忘記，我只是以歌當歌，表達我對自然，文化和人最基本的思想和感悟，在真切的生活體味中潛伏我的指紋和心跡，道出紀念碑，街坊的名字和地址。作為今人，我們應只爭朝夕，盡心盡力，為了書本和新天地，人人都應該幹一番大事業。

　禮尚往來的鄰居們呷著茶，口口念頌，「迷戀文字的人終將毀入文字」。這是真理，你信不信？

　在秋天的大道上，宣言聚攏，被囚禁的盲人，如金果，紛紛墜入秋天的河裡，我的善良又苛求的讀者！

米家路
1986年5月24日
於重慶歌樂山下

Author

Mi Jialu (original name Jiayan Mi) is the author of *Self-Fashioning and Reflexive Modernity in Modern Chinese Poetry, 1919-1949* (2004) and *Chinese Ecocinema in the Age of Environmental Challenge* (2009, co-edited with Sheldon Lu) and the editor of *Poetry Across Oceans: An Anthology of Chinese American Diaspora Poetry* (2014); *The Dao and the Routes: Mirage and Transfiguration in East-West Poetics* (2017) and *The Dao and the Routes: Enchantment and Spectrality in East-West Poetics* (2017). He is completing a book project in English titled "Heteroscape: Topography and Poetics of Navigation in Modern Chinese literature, Art and Film" to be published by Brill.

A graduate of Beijing University (MA), the Chinese University of Hong Kong (Ph. D) and the University of California at Davis (Ph. D), he is Associate Professor in the departments of English and World Languages & Cultures at The College of New Jersey. He lives in Princeton with his family.

語言文學類　PG2054　秀詩人53

深呼吸：
米家路中英對照詩選 1981-2018

作　　　者 / 米家路（Mi Jialu）
譯　　　者 / Jennifer Feeley、Matt Turner、Lucas Klein、Michael Day and Feng Yi
責任編輯 / 徐佑驊
圖文排版 / 林宛榆
封面設計 / 蔡瑋筠

發 行 人 / 宋政坤
法律顧問 / 毛國樑　律師
出版發行 / 秀威資訊科技股份有限公司
　　　　　114台北市內湖區瑞光路76巷65號1樓
　　　　　電話：+886-2-2796-3638　傳真：+886-2-2796-1377
　　　　　http://www.showwe.com.tw
劃撥帳號 / 19563868　戶名：秀威資訊科技股份有限公司
　　　　　讀者服務信箱：service@showwe.com.tw
展售門市 / 國家書店（松江門市）
　　　　　104台北市中山區松江路209號1樓
　　　　　電話：+886-2-2518-0207　傳真：+886-2-2518-0778
網路訂購 / 秀威網路書店：https://store.showwe.tw
　　　　　國家網路書店：https://www.govbooks.com.tw

2019年3月　BOD一版
定價：520元
版權所有　翻印必究
本書如有缺頁、破損或裝訂錯誤，請寄回更換

國家圖書館出版品預行編目

深呼吸：米家路中英對照詩選1981-2018/ 米家路
作；Jennifer Feeley等譯. -- 一版. -- 臺北
市：秀威資訊科技, 2019.03
　　面；　公分. -- (語言文學類；PG2054)(秀詩
人；53)
　BOD版
　ISBN 978-986-326-661-7(平裝)

851.486　　　　　　　　　　108001769

讀者回函卡

感謝您購買本書，為提升服務品質，請填妥以下資料，將讀者回函卡直接寄回或傳真本公司，收到您的寶貴意見後，我們會收藏記錄及檢討，謝謝！如您需要了解本公司最新出版書目、購書優惠或企劃活動，歡迎您上網查詢或下載相關資料：http:// www.showwe.com.tw

您購買的書名：＿＿＿＿＿＿＿＿＿＿＿＿＿＿＿＿＿＿＿＿＿＿＿

出生日期：＿＿＿＿＿年＿＿＿＿＿月＿＿＿＿＿日

學歷：□高中 (含) 以下　　□大專　　□研究所 (含) 以上

職業：□製造業　□金融業　□資訊業　□軍警　□傳播業　□自由業
　　　□服務業　□公務員　□教職　　□學生　□家管　　□其它＿＿＿＿

購書地點：□網路書店　□實體書店　□書展　□郵購　□贈閱　□其他

您從何得知本書的消息？

　□網路書店　□實體書店　□網路搜尋　□電子報　□書訊　□雜誌
　□傳播媒體　□親友推薦　□網站推薦　□部落格　□其他＿＿＿＿＿＿

您對本書的評價：(請填代號　1.非常滿意　2.滿意　3.尚可　4.再改進)

　封面設計＿＿＿　版面編排＿＿＿　內容＿＿＿　文／譯筆＿＿＿　價格＿＿＿

讀完書後您覺得：

□很有收穫　□有收穫　□收穫不多　□沒收穫

對我們的建議：＿＿＿＿＿＿＿＿＿＿＿＿＿＿＿＿＿＿＿＿＿＿＿

＿＿＿＿＿＿＿＿＿＿＿＿＿＿＿＿＿＿＿＿＿＿＿＿＿＿＿＿＿＿＿

＿＿＿＿＿＿＿＿＿＿＿＿＿＿＿＿＿＿＿＿＿＿＿＿＿＿＿＿＿＿＿

＿＿＿＿＿＿＿＿＿＿＿＿＿＿＿＿＿＿＿＿＿＿＿＿＿＿＿＿＿＿＿

11466
台北市內湖區瑞光路 76 巷 65 號 1 樓

秀威資訊科技股份有限公司　　　收

BOD 數位出版事業部

....

（請沿線對折寄回，謝謝！）

姓　　名：＿＿＿＿＿＿＿　年齡：＿＿＿　性別：□女　□男

郵遞區號：□□□□□

地　　址：＿＿＿＿＿＿＿＿＿＿＿＿＿＿＿＿＿

聯絡電話：(日) ＿＿＿＿＿＿＿　(夜) ＿＿＿＿＿＿＿

E-mail：＿＿＿＿＿＿＿＿＿＿＿＿＿＿＿＿＿